SPECIAL MESSAGE TO READERS

This book is published under the auspices of

THE ULVERSCROFT FOUNDATION

(registered charity No. 264873 UK)

Established in 1972 to provide funds for research, diagnosis and treatment of eye diseases. Examples of contributions made are: —

A Children's Assessment Unit at Moorfield's Hospital, London.

•

Twin operating theatres at the Western Ophthalmic Hospital, London.

•

A Chair of Ophthalmology at the Royal Australian College of Ophthalmologists.

•

The Ulverscroft Children's Eye Unit at the Great Ormond Street Hospital For Sick Children, London.

You can help further the work of the Foundation by making a donation or leaving a legacy. Every contribution, no matter how small, is received with gratitude. Please write for details to:

THE ULVERSCROFT FOUNDATION,
The Green, Bradgate Road, Anstey,
Leicester LE7 7FU, England.
Telephone: (0116) 236 4325

In Australia write to:
THE ULVERSCROFT FOUNDATION,
c/o The Royal Australian and New Zealand
College of Ophthalmologists,
94-98 Chalmers Street, Surry Hills,
N.S.W. 2010, Australia

Mogue Doyle has been in the building trade most of his life. He and his family live in Co. Wexford, Ireland.

DOWN A ROAD ALL REBELS RUN

West Wexford, 1920. Jim Rowe is the captain of a company of volunteers intent on fighting for their country's freedom. But they have to face the most ferocious of enemies, the Black and Tans, who are under strict orders to quell any notions of Irish independence among the local population. Jim is young, idealistic and committed. He starts to plan a big operation, but his dreams of success turn to fear when he suspects that one of his comrades may not be entirely loyal to the cause. When the Tans come after him, their reprisal is more vicious and more personal than he could ever have imagined.

Books by Mogue Doyle
Published by The House of Ulverscroft:

A MOTH AT THE GLASS

MOGUE DOYLE

DOWN A ROAD ALL REBELS RUN

Complete and Unabridged

ULVERSCROFT
Leicester

First published in Great Britain in 2005 by
Bantam Press, a division of
Transworld Publishers
London

First Large Print Edition
published 2005
by arrangement with
Transworld Publishers, a division of
The Random House Group Limited
London

All the characters in this book are fictitious and any resemblance to actual persons, living or dead, is purely coincidental.

British Library CIP Data

Doyle, Mogue
Down a road all rebels run.—Large print ed.—
Ulverscroft large print series: general fiction
1. Ireland—History—War of Independence,
1919 – 1921 —Fiction 2. Historical fiction
3. Large type books
I. Title
823.9′2 [F]

ISBN 1–84395–921–6

Published by
F. A. Thorpe (Publishing)
Anstey, Leicestershire

Set by Words & Graphics Ltd.
Anstey, Leicestershire
Printed and bound in Great Britain by
T. J. International Ltd., Padstow, Cornwall

This book is printed on acid-free paper

1

I'm telling you now, Lucy Brien, pondering is less bother than speechifying, and to take action is easier still. This was your motto too, even though you never said as much. It was also how things were in times gone by; certainly for those of us who fought and drove the old enemy from our land, stealth and silence were like brother and sister.

By 1920, that enemy had ears in every village and all conversations had become dangerous: one word in the wrong place could betray the best-laid plans and send men to their ends, unnecessarily. Instead, silence became our friend and we embraced her; seduced her till she blossomed into a lover — if you could answer me, Lucy Brien, you'd have something to say about that, with your dark hair low across your forehead and flowing down your shoulders like torrents of water down the sides of Scullogue Gap, and held it well too, you did, right to the end. But old men's ways of seeing things and their longstanding taste for silence aren't easily overhauled; fifty years on, I'm still reluctant to speak of certain matters or about most of the past — one topic only leads to blether of another.

So I could do with a helping hand here, Lucy my girl. Lately, our daughter has been asking — no, pestering me — about the Trouble Times. I tried to put her off by advising her to check the history books and read from those who were less reticent to relate their experiences. But Sarah is a persistent lady — like her mother — and I ended up telling her a few things, nothing specific, about the Tan War, 1919 to 1921; nothing she wouldn't find out about in one of those books.

I told her how our nation and culture had to be rescued before they were finally wiped out, and put back in their proper places among those of the great civilizations. How my father's generation had grown so used to British dominion that almost all sense of national identity had vanished, as had the pride and quality of taste that identity brings; even our very language, the odd time it was used to address a meeting or function, sounded foreign. His generation had gorged on the tittle-tattle of English Sunday newspapers, and flocked to the towns' theatres, where third-rate strolling companies and fifth-rate music-hall troupes would come to perform — and mostly they were English.

How our noble ideals, from the time of Parnell onwards, had fallen away, and that only a few people who'd recognized the situation were willing to do something.

By starting the Gaelic League movement, I said, Douglas Hyde had tried to restore our language and culture, and Arthur Griffith had set up the more politically minded Sinn Féin. But these groups had become just the foundations, not the revival itself, and, despite all the growing organizations and their pontificating, nothing much was to change till the 1916 Rising, when a small group of Volunteers rebelled in Dublin. The rebellion itself didn't amount to much; at least not until the commander of the British troops in Ireland, Maxwell, decided to teach the Irish a lesson they would never forget. In the course of a few days, he had fifteen of the rebel leaders shot. But his action had the opposite effect: as men unknown to us before were being turned into martyrs, their heroism became the spur we had badly needed, and everything began to change quickly, utterly.

So began the dream of freedom, I told Sarah. It seeped through to every young fellow with guts and spleen, and we grew passionate about a new way of life. There was a sudden interest in history, and at night we cycled to town for Irish-language classes; the real revival at last was under way. Some of us, though, who believed we'd have to fight for our dream, joined the Irish Volunteers — and if at times we were, maybe, a touch profane when one or two things unbecoming had to be carried out, it was all for the sacred cause of freedom. Yes, freedom was the offspring of stealth and silence, and my generation was the midwife there to oversee its gestation and help with the birth throes.

It seems, however, that none of this will satisfy Sarah's curiosity: she keeps asking for more information. So, Lucy Brien, what choice do I have but to take a leaf out of your book? I can almost hear the tone of your voice saying: Simply tell her what happened, the good side and the bad. Whether we want to disclose it or not, you say, her generation has a right to know what went on in the Trouble Times.

As difficult as it is to tell her about my involvement as a Volunteer, when Sarah asks about the hand, act and part of a certain other individual during our fight for freedom her words come as a jolt to the system. For heaven's sake, why does she want to know anything about the likes of that fellow Rutch Kelly . . . ?

* * *

The first time I had a bit of a barney with Rutch Kelly was back in January 1919.

That Monday night, a group of men had gathered illegally in the back yard outside Murphy's bar and were standing around, talking in half-whispers. Behind turned-up collars, their faces were barely recognizable in the glow of an oil lamp through the back window of the bar. The stars sparkled in the heavens, while in my thoughts the black mountain behind us was as massive as a bent colossus rising from the dark earth, crying out for blood, more blood — and the one thing about young men is their willingness to spill it; all they need is a cause.

Except on that occasion, there was good common cause between us. The word *freedom* seemed to shimmer across the constellations overhead. Not that there was anything new about that age-old dream, but to an impatient young man almost on fire with vehemence it had become a fresh vision, shining. Little more than a year before, I had joined the Irish Volunteers to fight for my nation's full independence — with no half-measures, any more, of Home Rule or regional government. Neither man nor beast would get in the way of that quest.

An old pal had just walked over to me, and as the light from the window of the bar caught the whites of his eyes, there was no doubt but he had something serious on his mind. When he opened his mouth to speak, there was even less doubt but that Mylie Byrne was about to ask for something, or for me to do him a favour.

The previous weekend, the leader of our company of Volunteers, Nowlan, had accidentally shot himself while attending training camp near Davis' Mills. If he hadn't, somebody sooner or later would've put a bullet in him. The members of the company were called to assemble the following night when the brigade commandant would come from town, inspect us and announce our new leader. Having served as Nowlan's lieutenant, Rutch Kelly no doubt expected to be the automatic choice. But things didn't turn out that way.

Before any announcement, Volunteer Mylie Byrne and a group of men had held a meeting with the brigade officer — a vice-commandant attended instead of the CO, who'd been sent abroad to buy arms. They'd refused to accept Rutch Kelly as their leader. A number of incidents were cited, where both himself and the wounded captain had led us, that were totally at odds with the aims of the Volunteer movement.

These incidents had taken place after

Christmas and into the New Year. We'd just got word that our company would have to arm and kit itself out without assistance from either brigade headquarters in our local town or from general headquarters in Dublin. What we had was an army without weapons, equipment or the money to buy them. GHQ in Dublin had also said that if arms became available we still wouldn't get any, because, when the military campaign started in earnest throughout the land, our own county would play no major role: its geographical layout was unsuitable for the sort of tactics they had in mind. All available rifles and support, outside of Dublin's needs, were going to be diverted to Munster — the campaign organizer's own personal bailiwick. That was the word. The message, though, had been made clear: we were part of a Volunteer army in name only. On offer were instructions, guidelines and plenty of old talk, but not a revolver, haversack or bandolier, not so much as one blooming pair of puttees even, would they give us. It was up to ourselves to take on the fight, and we could go whistle for guns.

So the leaders of our unit had set about arming themselves. A list had been drawn up — barracks, demesnes, addresses of soldiers in the Great War, which had just ended, and all those likely to have had a rifle, fowling piece, shotgun or any small arms in their houses. One of the first places to be hit was a merchant's house, eight miles away, on this side of town. Being a Loyalist, with two sons who served in the British Army, there was a good chance he'd have a few guns in the house. But as easy as the job was, Nowlan and Kelly, along with two others, had managed to make a hames of it.

First they sent two young boys to the door with an urgent message that the man's premises on Main Street, in town, were on fire. The merchant was out. The boys then asked if his sons were home from the war yet: might they do something? There were no men inside. About five minutes later, our fellows went knocking on the door. When the maid again answered, they brushed past her into the hall. The merchant's wife came from the kitchen when she heard the commotion, whereupon the bold Rutch Kelly stuck a pistol against her forehead and ordered her to put her hands up. She refused, and shouted back at a girl in the kitchen to get the workman outside to go for the police. Her bluff — the workman had gone home long before — and her defiance were too much for our leaders, and they duly panicked. On their way out, they pulled two old swords and a dagger off the wall — by heavens, we'd take on the might of the British Empire with shagging ornaments. The next day, the constabulary collected what our boys had missed — a pair of rifles, a service revolver and a shotgun — and brought them to the barracks for safekeeping.

The second incident quoted to the commandant was the robbery of a lady from the next parish. Rutch Kelly and two of his cronies in the unit had stopped the woman on her road home, her bicycle laden with shopping. The pistol was again produced and she was relieved of her belongings. Later, they opened the parcels and found items of women's personal wear — all in the colour mauve — among other things. A new tactic of war, then? Dressed in mauve bloomers and brandishing ornaments, we'd frighten the British out of Ireland. News of our company's escapades spread, and smart alecks of shopkeepers in town, when they heard, said: We'd have been safer in France with Redmond in the trenches, before Armistice Day, than hereabouts with the Bloomer Men on the loose. Till then, our unit had been called the Hill Men.

So before the vice-commandant of the county's north brigade could tell us who our new captain would be, he'd have some serious sorting out to do. Having inspected the unit, he gave us a dressing down.

The behaviour of this brigade company, says he, shamed him. Rather than disband, the unit would get one more chance, and the Volunteers would elect their own leader. The brigade would endorse the new captain, and this unit would fit in properly with the chain of command. Each Volunteer would familiarize himself with the rules and ideals of the movement, attend regular drill and become a disciplined soldier. Mavericks would be shot — if the necessary bullets could only be found.

Letting us get on with the job of electing our new leader, the vice-commandant had gone into Murphy's bar to wait.

As Mylie Byrne began quietly, but intently, speaking to me, a few other men who'd talked earlier to the brigade officer about a new leader came up behind him. It was as if they appeared out of nowhere, or had risen from the earth. There was such unease in the place, and stealth, that I was more interested in their arrival — its suddenness — than in the strange proposal Mylie Byrne was putting to me.

Had the vice-commandant not foreseen this situation, I wondered. Though only an amateur like the rest of us, he should've thought things through and made it his business to do the job himself. When a man volunteered, he took a pledge to carry out orders and fight for his country, not to go around drumming up votes. We were a group of part-time soldiers in need of direction, not some political party whose leadership was voted on; as if our land hadn't suffered enough down the years from dabblers in politics!

Grand parliamentarians, 105 Irish MPs per term trucking and trading in Westminster, had failed to lay their hands on the least form of Home Rule, and the Irish Parliamentary Party had been almost wiped out in the December 1918 elections. Surely it was now time to turf out that useless shower of officials above in Dublin Castle — to clear out the whole system? There since the Act of Union in 1800, they were supposed to be managing the country, but the system and its officials were a disaster. It wasn't just a *new* government we wanted: our country needed its own *sovereign* government.

We'd handed the political side of our movement over to Sinn Féin, and I was keen to see how it would do after its big victory in the December polling. But Mylie Byrne was the real one for the politics. He knew all about Arthur Griffith, the man who'd founded Sinn Féin, and about Griffith's ideas for Irish nationality as set out in his paper *The United Irishman*.

Though he was a year or more older than me, many a time I'd saved Mylie Byrne from being mauled in the schoolyard — even then he wasn't afraid to needle the boys who'd ganged together to control the school terrain. And I'd had to go to his rescue again afterwards, in 1915, one Fair Day in town. While waiting for my father to finish his dealings with the buyer of our few sheep, I went down the town to stretch my legs. Mylie Byrne, with his arms round a bundle of pamphlets, was walking up the street towards me. The pamphlets fell and scattered on the pavement when two peelers came from behind and grabbed him. I ran down, knocked the cap off one fellow and clobbered him with my blackthorn stick. When Mylie kneed the other fellow in the groin, I used my free hand to box the bent-over figure to the pavement. Mylie panicked and wanted to flee town towards home, but I caught him by the elbow and steered him in the other direction. Better not to lead them out our road, I said. Let's hang around to see what happens.

I led him down the street and into a haberdashery shop out of harm's way. Having told the ladies behind the counter we were entertainers in town for the day, I demanded a few yards of fabric to cover ourselves with so we could ply our trade around town, adding that we'd return that evening to pay our bill. No doubt the ladies didn't believe us, but thought it wiser to agree — especially when we glowered and gurned a little. So they pinned and tied lengths of red and black cotton to each of us, and pieces of tweed as shawls — and lower that fellow's dress to hide his big feet, I said.

So two old crones, one hobbling with a blackthorn stick, left the shop and floundered around the Square. While savouring the sight of peelers questioning young men, we complained to elderly women out and about of the cruelty in policemen's hearts, the damp and the old pains in our bones. As Mylie Byrne tightened his waist, a pamphlet, *Ireland, Germany and the Freedom of the Seas* by Roger Casement, fell to the ground. I snatched it up from under his skirt, went across the street to hand it to one of the peelers, and pointed out to him where the lads who'd given me the pamphlet had gone. Thank you, mam, says he, and a half-dozen Royal Irish Constabulary scuttled off down the town. That incident had happened four years previous.

⋆ ⋆ ⋆

Though the meeting in the back yard had begun at seven in the evening, time went by on a slow drip, and the two hours to nine o'clock — the agreed period allowed for canvassing and drumming up support before the voting would eventually begin — were like a priest's wake, dry and dreary. The late January frost bit through our topcoats as we stamped on the hard ground and cross-slapped our arms to keep warm. Orion stomped across the sky, sword held sparkling aloft, and he waved that shield not so much at the bull before him as at our dawdling.

Despite the cold, a sniff of hops from empty oak casks nearby was enough to taunt our nostrils with sweet temptation. By hook or by crook, before the night was out we'd see the inside of the window, where the brigade officer at that moment was sitting — the privileges of the brass — under a poster of someone, not unlike himself, with no right to be there. In the meantime, all we could do was dream ahead: of a modicum of comfort; of whiffs and flavours titillating our nostrils while we stared at bottles along the back shelves, and not a dead-man among them; of the eye being mesmerized by tumblers placed on the counter during that special moment of critical delay before the malt-infused gold would caress — but first sting a little, like a woman playing hard to get. Dream of how the flavour would gently wash against the taste buds round the mouth; of sitting down at last and imagining barley fields in August, two horses before a binder round a brow to keep the malthouses going for at least one more year, so we might return to sip and dream ahead again, gazing through shiny, diamond-sparkled glass that twinkled like the Swordsman of the Sky above.

It didn't bother me who was to become captain. If Rutch Kelly had been appointed, I'd have accepted it as a fact and then used my wits to deal with any situation in which his orders became too much, or his manner overbearing. But this whole rigmarole was overly drawn out, and Mylie Byrne's game of politics-by-stealth too self-indulgent for my liking, for the job could've been over and done with, and we'd have long since gone inside for that drop of malt. But when he was caught in the light all of a sudden, the intent on his face, and on the others', jerked me back like I was being pulled from behind by the coat-tails. And I was no longer indifferent to his low voice, or to the plan he was laying out before me.

Rowe, we'd like you to take on the job, Mylie Byrne said. His low voice was so deliberate the words were like knives.

What? Are you fellows out to make a fool of me? says I.

No, we're not trying to make a fool of you, was the reply.

They were serious all right: their looks stayed fixed, not a budge, and their insistent proposal hung there, hassling me.

The unit needs a good overhaul, Mylie said. Discipline, for a start, has to be sorted out. We have neither equipment nor arms, except one or two revolvers — fellows' own pieces. The standard of drill is poor; regular training is vital. The movement countrywide is being stepped up a gear to become more of a threat to the Crown forces in Ireland. The boys in Dublin are serious. We'll have to fight; become wanted men. The captain will have to give instructions and plan ambushes.

And issue orders to attack and kill, I said, finishing his little speech for him.

But it didn't stop Mylie from talking. We need somebody strong the men can look up to, says he, who can think on his feet and has some bit of decency about him. I've seen you in action: you're the only one in this company with the ability to lead us.

I'm nineteen years old, for feck sake, I said. How do you expect men going on thirty, not to mention the likes of Rutch Kelly there, to take orders from a nineteen-year-old? But my worst fear was not about getting fellows, mostly older than me, to follow orders; it was of not knowing enough to carry the job — and this job could go on for months, years.

Rutch Kelly is only about your own age, says Mylie Byrne. And most of us won't serve under him — would *you* take orders from him? So it's either that or have the company stood down.

Why don't you take on the job yourself? I says.

You know very well that Rutch Kelly won't accept that, says Mylie. Especially when he hears that I've blocked his claim for leadership. And if he goes from the unit, he'll take enough of his cronies with him to leave the group too small to carry on — with thirty men, we're few enough as it is.

Look, says he, here's the plan. At the start, I'll run against Kelly and cause a split in the vote. This stalemate will drag on till we're blue in the face and there's no way out. By then, the men will be so fed up, they'll either agree on a compromise candidate or accept that the company be stood down. One way or another Kelly will have to give up his designs on the job. He'll have no choice but to settle for someone else. I'll arrange for a Volunteer to put your name forward at that stage — with luck, Kelly won't know the idea came from me. He'll surely agree to accept you, rather than disband.

You're presuming an awful lot there, Byrne, for this scheme to work, says I. How long is it going to drag on for? Will we get inside for even one drink?

But I couldn't say I didn't pleasure my pride a little: the idea of being top dog in the local Volunteers. Get up from the fire and let Mr Rowe sit down. Or, I'll be with you there in a minute; can't you see I'm pouring a drink for the captain. Oh yes, Mr Rowe, right away, sir.

Suddenly caught in the light just then, the face of one, Rutch Kelly, interrupted my moment of indulgence, and gratification changed to trepidation.

⋆ ⋆ ⋆

As Mylie Byrne had predicted, both he and Kelly went head to head in the race for leadership. Mylie had more support, but not the two-thirds majority required to get elected and avoid a split. Both men then put forward plans and propositions, but all to no avail. The stalemate only hardened, like the frost under our feet.

At one point Kelly scoffed at Byrne and challenged him to a boxing match to settle the matter. Byrne knew better than to heed the taunt — I wasn't so sure that it was only a taunt. We were at a standstill. Unless somebody soon came up with a new suggestion, we'd have to give up the idea of picking a leader ourselves and let the brass sort it out — the way it should've been, to begin. A boot stamped on a frozen puddle of water, and the crunch of ice sounded strangely in keeping with the growing frustration.

Eventually a fellow, who up to then had supported Kelly, called to be heard: he had a proposal to make — the first sign of Mylie Byrne's scheme, and, right enough, he was a politician. But my admiration for his talent became tempered as a shiver went down my spine.

Rutch Kelly looked enormous in the window light. Jolly and ruddy like the face on the poster inside on the wall, and his frame was as powerful, surely, as a gorilla's. No wonder fellows were afraid of him. Only when old Murphy inside sent us out a lit hurricane lamp did the menace of Kelly's presence reduce slightly.

Not that he bullied his cronies with brute force; his tactics, I knew, were usually more controlled. Kelly could use dread like a well-practised weapon in his hands, and the inkling of violence was enough to give fellows the shakes. Yet his style was almost flamboyant, with a certain flair that was hard not to marvel at. He was some spectacle in operation.

Nine o'clock had come and gone, with an even denser fog off our breaths. Kelly's gang seemed a comfortable and safe place to be. I was tempted to drop Mylie Byrne's damned scheme, go over and tell your man a dirty yarn and have him put his big arm round my shoulder. I'd snort out laughing at nothing with the others and mope about under Kelly's protection. Life would be so much easier.

I was on the brink of becoming leader of a company in a rebel army: what had I let myself in for? An untrained unit, without equipment or arms — many of us had never even got the feel of a rifle. On top of that, six or seven of the thirty-odd in the group were no more than louts under the thumb of a pug-nosed hooligan. Some rebel group we were, in search of a noble cause. Without a soldier's experience of battle to draw on, or any great nineteenth-century Fenian tradition in my blood — no rebel background whatever — how would a fellow handle the likes of them?

2

As a boy growing up, I'd heard the old people tell stories of our ancestors, and had learned how my forefathers had been cowed, too put down to dare lift their heads to wish for a better life — unless prepared to uproot and go to America. When a storyteller spoke of the ancient longing for freedom that'd always been part of our make-up I felt the same yearning. That feeling developed, and was nurtured into a passion: the vehement need to remove the markings of St Patrick from the Union Jack. And when the storyteller told us about Jer Tobin, a mountain neighbour of ours who'd crawled on his hands and knees across the floor to Mr Lloyd, the landlord's agent, at the sittings of the Land Commission back in 1882, and begged to have his rent settled, you'd feel a certain bile stir inside you.

My father, however, had just a bare interest in who ruled the country, and my mother had even less. Too busy keeping body and soul together, they were, surviving off a layer of soil that little more than covered the hill rock to have time to dabble in such a trivial thing as politics. Matters of life and death were foremost in the minds of most families who lived on the Blackstairs mountain.

My older brother, Ben, and I had scarcely made it three days a week to primary school in the village, and our youngest brother, Paddy, seldom saw the inside of a classroom. He might leave home in the morning, but nobody knew where he went or how he spent his day. The school-attendance man rarely bothered us; the trip to the school was probably enough for him, without having to traipse across heather and commons and chase hares the likes of Paddy Rowe. So the lad never learned to read and write, but could he find his way round the mountain and run like a crazy elk? Far from afternoon levees, garden fêtes and interest in hustings we were reared.

If my father'd had any leanings at all in politics, it would've been towards his fellow county-man, Redmond, whose aim was Home Rule won fairly and squarely by parliamentary means over in Westminster. He'd had no interest in uprisings, gatherings-by-stealth in the moonlight or any of that Fenianism caper. Irish rebellion, in his view, caused nothing but strife and left terrible consequences in its wake: pure horror and the purging of ordinary people from their homes.

Like what'd happened in the aftermath of 1798 — at least thirty thousand people were killed on the island in that war — and so numbed was our county's spirit that, during the following century, generations even refused to speak of '98.

My father's one great desire, ever, had been to own the sweet — mean, more like — bit of mountain soil, the twenty acres that put food on his table, where his grandfather before him, having been evicted back in 1836 from an adjoining estate lower down, had come and settled. It would take three generations of Rowes, at constant war with the wilderness, to knock into shape this unreclaimed, unfenced patch of mountain, with neither house nor outhouse to sleep in. And yet the holding still wasn't theirs: rent had to be paid — and on time.

Things got better, though. The passing of the Wyndham Land Act, in the English Parliament of 1903, gave Irish farmers the means to buy up, at reasonable prices, the land they farmed but hadn't owned since the time of Cromwell. And my father became a happy man.

When Edward VII and his wife, Alexandra, visited the country the same year, it was like the newly crowned pair had brought my father his own special gold parchment, with

Land Act written across the top. He would for ever be in their debt, he told us, and certainly wouldn't stand for any political campaigning outside of what was allowed by the Parliamentary Party and its leader, John Redmond. No reason why the royals shouldn't have a pleasant trip and a bit of a welcome, as a gesture for giving him back his rights.

When a handful of mean-spirited whingers in Dublin had objected to the visit, he was disgusted, especially with that one, Maud Gonne, who'd hung a black petticoat from her window to mark the occasion; as if she and her lot — of the same upper-crust breeding as the royals — had ever been oppressed or evicted. That hussy, the privileges of the world at her feet, had no place pulling such a stunt; she and that other troublemaker, Arthur Griffith, didn't represent him and the small farmers he knew.

The old man would go on about it for years afterwards, and as peace slipped away and strife started once more, he'd say: It all began when that woman, Gonne, hung her undergarment out the window, and it wasn't the first time, either, that there was mischief over a petticoat — and most certainly not the last time, as I'd find out for myself over the following years.

My mother, a woman of nearly six feet, would give him a look that softened his tirade. I didn't understand then her effect upon him, or the sway she could hold, when the notion took her: she'd always been as meek as a mouse with her three sons. Oddly enough, watching Rutch Kelly's antics reminded me of her. All she'd had to do was throw that look or rise suddenly from her stool, without even a word, and the world would go hush.

Sinn Féin, the old man had laughed at the good of it. Sinn Féin — We Are It, or so the schoolmaster in the village was supposed to have told him. Nothing like being cocksure of themselves anyway, says he. I'd heard the same schoolmaster say Sinn Féin simply meant We Ourselves. Other people, in their conversations, were not so caustic about this new movement. My mother too, when I checked it with her, seemed less biased against them: she just shrugged and said nothing.

At sixteen years of age in 1916, my interest in the state of our nation had increased all of a sudden. It wasn't so much the hopeless bravery of a small group of men and women — a dour enough way to go into any fight — but their audacity that I admired, in taking on the might of an empire. The lesson the rebels had taught me was: it's a better-quality and more wholesome existence, however short, to be free and able to dream, and even become a touch brash, than to live a good long life as a demure, second-class citizen of some other realm, no matter how great. I'd begun to dream of independence for ourselves, and to look around at whichever movements might work best towards that end.

You could all but feel the desire for change among the young people. We got impatient with the staid politics of the Parliamentary Party, especially with the older generation's trust in its leader — John Redmond appeared to be more of a recruiting agent for the British Army than an advocate for the needs and changing expectations of his own people. So we looked elsewhere for ideas and guidance. While Sinn Féin hadn't been responsible for the 1916 Rising — which had been the work of the Irish Volunteers and the Irish Citizen Army mostly — it was the group that made the most progress afterwards, and branches sprang up throughout the country. Its aims, of course, were to achieve an independent Ireland, but the party seemed to represent small businessmen and farmers more than the interests of other groups. The odd thing was that Mylie Byrne, the employee of a small businessman and whose welfare the party didn't really cater for, took to Sinn Féin like a lark to a clear morning sky. It was only natural that I, too, should join. Yet as soon as my initial curiosity had been gratified, my enthusiasm waned: for some reason, I couldn't warm to the workings of the party, or to its manoeuvrings.

Anyway, what would Sinn Féin achieve by not taking up their seats in Westminster, following the December 1918 elections? And while it was all very well to have our own national government as a counterpart to London's, what odds would it make if we couldn't enforce the laws passed? Far-reaching changes, it seemed to me, could only be brought about by much more drastic action. After the British had executed the leaders of the 1916 Rising, our ancient race demanded not only retribution but full satisfaction also, through freedom in a new republic. I then joined the Irish Volunteers and found their aim — achievement of that republic by force — to be much more direct and to my liking.

So that was the reason I was standing there in the frost behind Murphy's pub, waiting to have my name put forward as leader. A good enough reason, too, not to slink away from the burden of being captain, and let the unit be disbanded.

⋆ ⋆ ⋆

And who is it you have in mind? says Rutch Kelly. What's the name of this compromise candidate? Come, tell us; the wait is killing me.

His voice had nothing if not contempt. Steel-blue eyes scanned us to see who would have the gall to step forward and challenge him, or dare put their hands on his legacy. Imagine a person among us, other than Mylie Byrne, who'd even think of issuing Kelly with the smallest instruction. Indeed, could anyone present defy him so much as to think of another name, never mind propose it?

Well, one man could. Young Jerry Tobin, whose father had pleaded on his knees not to have his rent increased, the man who up till then had supported Kelly for leadership, got everybody's attention when he spoke out. And, fair play to him, he didn't flinch.

Since we've ground to a halt and can't decide between Rutch Kelly and Mylie Byrne, says he, I'd like to try and break the jam. I think we should select a neutral candidate, a third person, who doesn't belong in either camp. And so, to unite our company,

I propose James Rowe as the compromise candidate.

On hearing it called out so formally I felt removed from my name, as if it was somebody else's, especially as it came from Jerry Tobin — a fellow I'd thought of as one of Kelly's toadies. Once again, though, I had to admire Mylie Byrne's shrewdness. The old schemer! He'd stage-managed the whole show: arranged for Tobin to support Kelly in order to pull the rug from under him at the final hurdle.

But Mr Kelly wasn't going to give in easily. Mad as a must elephant, he rose from his hunkers and pushed his way to the front of the group around him. And Jerry Tobin was going to be the butt of his rage. Kelly's big fist went up and out, as if he was about to demolish the small man. Instead he controlled his *taom*: his forefinger slowly reached Tobin's forehead, puckered the flesh as it traced a line across it, then continued down the bridge of the nose to rest on the lips. The act held more contempt than a box in the mouth. And then the finishing touches: he gripped Tobin's lips between the vice of his finger and thumb.

Mylie Byrne seemed to come from nowhere and stood beside me. The right pocket of my greatcoat felt heavy, as though a stone had been dropped in.

Here, says he quietly, fit that on for size. It might come in handy before much longer. Only, when you use it, try not to let it be seen, or all the lads will want them.

The piece of metal with holes to take fingers was warm: Mylie Byrne must've had it on his hand all the while. A precaution he'd taken against the vagaries of the night — he must've thought he no longer needed it, and that I did. Mylie's hunch was a worrying one, because of his accuracy in anticipating the course of events till then — predicting where the ghouls of the dark might focus their devilry next.

Rutch Kelly wasn't finished with Jer Tobin. His two arms rose in the air. Coming down mightily on his victim's shoulders, he grabbed Tobin by the *scrogall*. There was a short wrestling match — or, rather, a throttling mismatch — and Tobin landed on his back. Kelly stood over him and rested a foot on his chest, like a circus elephant might do to its trainer. Something stirred in my gut, more in revulsion than anger. This was no longer a matter of two men having a scrap.

To me, Kelly's foot on the other man's chest meant something else. The way he stood, he even looked like a landlord, or the agent who'd bullied Tobin's father. The

Tobins, the Rowes and every family — what matter their names? — had all been bullied. The centuries of tyranny had us lying on our backs, pinned to the ground. My old man had cowered to a bearded old king — the landlord of all accursed landlords — in welcome, back in 1903, and I felt shame. No, it wasn't anger that was in my gut, but an overwhelming urge to retch. I couldn't hold it down any longer.

I put my right hand in my pocket and slipped onto my fingers the knuckleduster that Mylie Byrne had dropped in. Kelly's big head was in the air like a glorious victor as I stepped forward in his direction.

Get off that man, I said, trying to sound calm.

Kelly looked at me and scowled. Pure John Bull himself, in shape and size, he didn't even consider it worthwhile to make fun of my challenge. I was taller than him — at that moment I thanked my mother for my height — and, now that I'd crossed the first hurdle, I no longer felt so intimidated by his presence. I quickly got annoyed with myself, though. It doesn't do being too cocky: it would be all the easier to get caught with an unexpected clip and end up beside Tobin on the ground — I'd learned as much from scrapping with my brothers. Then came the charge.

It was more a lunge, really. All I had to do was jerk sideways at the last minute, out of Kelly's line of movement, and leave the toe of my boot slightly raised for him to stub against. He went by me like a bull, buffered against a group of fellows behind me and knocked a couple of them onto their backsides. It was a start.

Up he got and began another stumble-charge at me, then checked — fair play to him: he'd quickly learned that a more controlled approach was needed. He feigned another lunge, then instead threw an almighty swipe with his right, intending to knock my block off.

I ducked his blow. As if of its own accord, the knuckleduster tightened in my fist, and I got him right on the button with a neat uppercut. His head jerked back from the steel round my fingers, and there was a give to his jawbone, maybe even the sound of a crack — or was that wishful thinking? Down he went, but stumbled back onto his feet. This time I used my left to the solar plexus to stun him — those brothers of mine had known how to scrap — then I gave him a full dose of steel on the chin again.

Rutch Kelly dropped like an ugly sack.

But things couldn't be left unfinished. If I were to stamp my authority on his pack-pals

— a show of force was what they understood best — I'd have to let them see I could be as violent as their master, if not more so. And this was my chance.

I needed a knife. If Mylie Byrne carried a knuckle-duster, he might also have a knife. And as if by instinct, when I looked at him and made a gesture of a short stabbing movement, he pulled out a dagger and tossed it to me.

I waited the half-minute till Kelly came round and got to his knees. I went behind him, grabbed him by the hair and stuck my knee against his spine; then I pulled back his head and put the blade to his neck. A sigh of awe, a sort of horror, went up from the group. Mylie Byrne's was the only face with a sign of anything else: a smirk — satisfaction maybe — as his eyes fixed on Kelly's neck. He'd anticipated my next move while I was still figuring it out.

I kept the position, held the scene and milked it for its delirious rush of satisfaction. Pink flesh kissed the blade, while the beast — by then, more a pig than a bull; a fat pig pinned across a dray squealing out its last moments before getting stuck — was silent. There was a moment of temptation: to make the mark, draw the cross and prod. Every face, except Mylie Byrne's, was like a spectator's awaiting that decisive goal in a hurling match.

Instead I gave his neck a slight nick, to draw blood and put the wind up the others.

Kelly was still on his knees, in shock, as I let go and walked away. But I went off only an arm's length, spun round quickly, swung my fist and, with the heel of the dagger, gave him a tearing belt in the mouth. If his jaw wasn't broken before, it was now. A thousand wide-eyed mouths were transfixed, it seemed, shivering and gawping at me — an even worse terror than Rutch Kelly ever was.

Now, I roared, let's get on with what we have to do. I want to get inside for a ball of malt before the night's out.

I enjoyed hearing myself say that.

Overhead, Orion sparkled silver and kept on stomping across the sky, though to us mere mortals on the frozen ground it seemed he never budged.

3

You'd think by now, Lucy Brien, our daughter would've lost interest in events that took place over seventy years ago. But it seems she's got the stomach for bloody stories, and wants to hear more. To balance the picture somewhat, I tell her about some of the good times you and I had.

How we used to walk out, leaving the town behind us, when I'd call for you. To take in the fresh air of a September evening, how we'd stride for an hour or two through the Duffry, the Black Country, towards the mountain — there's nothing I would relish more this moment. On our way we'd cross the Bloody Bridge, pass through the Mile-house and climb up Monart hill. Because nobody else did, you blessed yourself passing the grave of William Reynells, a yeoman shot on Vinegar Hill in 1798 — no call bearing a grudge against the foe of our ancestors, you said. I've learned from you, and to this day, passing the same spot, I make the sign of the cross — more a salute from one old soldier to another than the observance of religious procedure. We used to listen outside Robert's

Forge for the sound of the ancient rhythm: shapes hammered, shapes made — remember the clink-clink clank? But that beat, I'm afraid, is also gone: the big man has changed over to the electric welder, while these days a broken gate sits propped against the silent anvil, a deconsecrated altar to the god of fire.

The first time ever we made that journey, Lucy my girl, we stopped at the Cutting Road further on — you remember the spot? That stretch of road had been built during the Famine, by the likes of my grandfather — an old man in a corner by the time I knew him — who broke stones to stave off starvation. Made a good road, he did, for the rest of us to walk on. We remained there a while in that hallowed place, one of many in the story of our tribe, to relish across our young faces the glorious rose-red of the sun going down, and looked back the way we'd come. Your coal-dark hair, as you lay on the ground, seemed to flow from your head to earth as if you were in sacred collusion with the forces beneath. I hesitated to touch you — it was a moment to behold and remember, rather than sully with desire. Defilement and reverence: always the two opposites tugging at a young man.

It was ever a delight to rest with you in the pastures of Colclough's vast estates. Their rich green would shine all the more brightly when a light shower had given late grass added sparkle, heaven-sent holy water to old roots — was there anything in the world to match the feel of soft rain after the harvest, or the sight of a distant bank of low mist along the Urrin valley? But when I talked of how all that land had once been black with oak, ash and *skeoch*, the ancient forest going back to the beginning, you weren't listening — no need for explanation: you understood it instinctively.

What's left of Killoughrim Wood is as defiant today as ever in the face of its executioners, like a proud elk on its knees and in the final throes. Time was when I could walk through the place with my eyes shut; many's the night our men had sheltered there while on the run. Wonder if it's still haunted. Then at last before the sun went down, I'd walk you home, with our backs to the old wood, the Cutting Road and the mountain.

When she was young, our daughter must've heard all this before from you: she has become impatient, and can hardly wait for me to return to the Troubles and tell her more about the activities of the Volunteers. Not only does she ask about Rutch Kelly, Sarah has begun to enquire about a certain lady as well. You don't mind, do you, if I tell her about that lady?

As a member of Cumann na mBan, the women's organization that took part in our nation's struggle for independence, Hannah Jordan was a vital link in our campaign during those years. And from the time I was appointed captain of our company, I had reason to be in contact with her and to call upon her for assistance. Her personal loyalties and allegiance to the cause were never in doubt, and even though we had other Volunteer units in the area her group in Cumann na mBan was always much more willing to help us.

* * *

A fortnight had passed since the episode behind Murphy's. Still without rifles, we had to use replicas shaped from boards, off-cuts Mylie Byrne had scavenged from the mill where he worked. Mylie'd got his friend Peter Pender, whose job there was in the grain lofts, to help him run off boards on the big bench-saw. They then cut them into four- or five-foot lengths — and two-by-two-inch sections on the small saw. It goes without saying, Mylie had tried many times to inveigle his pal into the Volunteers, but Peter was only ever interested in hurling, dancing and chasing the ladies. I'd sooner join the Clohamon Fife and Drum Band, says he. But get a few women into this army of yours and you'll have me marching up there the very next night. How about that?

The lengths of wood were left out in a pile, for each Volunteer to collect his own piece along with a triangular board to attach as a gunstock. The mock-up was modelled on the Lee-Enfield or Martini rifle — though what we ended up with weren't exactly the shapeliest of articles. But two pieces slotted together and bound by cord were easily dismantled whenever there was word of peelers — the Royal Irish Constabulary was beginning to get snoopy of late. And we'd immediately spread out across the field, to become the most genteel cricket team in the Empire.

Three stumps quickly stuck down with bails on top, one piece to bat and we'd throw the other timbers in the ditch — not that we knew much about cricket, but the peelers knew even less. The bike patrol would stop by the field gate to gawp like goats at a cliff edge. A young constable once asked if that was American baseball we were playing there. No it's German cricket, somebody shouted back. And the coppers moved off. In a way, I was relieved to see them: the men could release their bile against an entity outside their own unit, and afterwards the timbers were reassembled with an even greater resolve.

No matter how well a replica was shaped and sanded, though, it had nothing near the feel of the genuine article. Arms drill was a cod, almost off-putting: we were more a group of boys playing soldiers than men with intent. When the training officer barked out, *Present arms*, a low chorus of yowls would answer as fingers picked up splinters. Heaven save us if we'd ever have to contend with a hail of bullets or prods of bayonets. All the same, the lads understood and stuck with the job. It made a difference, too, that the fellow doing the drill was a right martinet, with a voice like a rasp.

Though Volunteer Tommy Doran had supported Rutch Kelly for the job of captain, I appointed Tommy company training officer for marching, close-order drill and arms drill. Having served in the British Army and seen the front in the Great War, he knew all about weapons. He had a way with the men too: they respected his knowledge and accepted the rigours he put them through. Though pals with Rutch Kelly, he wasn't one of his lackeys, and his loyalty came without question; there was no reason to mistrust him. As discipline and sharpness improved, there were signs of a new enthusiasm: the lads regularly attended training and turned up on time.

I even convinced my brother Paddy to join: the training would put a rein on his ways. Though he didn't turn up regularly at first, and would leave before the session was over, he was gradually broken in. He would remain living at home for some years, searching the mountain-side for dead animals to skin and sell to Michael Wilde in town. Then one morning he was gone — he'd told Ben he was going to sea — and we weren't to lay eyes on him again for a long time.

* * *

I thought a little diversion might do the men good. If their new captain were, say, to organize this entertainment himself and then indulge wholeheartedly, it ought to improve our rapport — remove the awkwardness between captain and men. To make the unit work, I needed to win over their confidence more and improve camaraderie.

Something else: I needed to work on Rutch Kelly and build bridges. Though we'd never become the best of pals, I'd have to get on with him; appeal to his better nature and soften his gall, so he'd at least tolerate me as leader. 'Twould take time: the worse the scalding, the longer the time to mend.

My biggest concern was preventing Kelly from getting revenge. Broken jaw or not, it didn't keep the brute away from drill, and I was nervous of turning my back on him for a second. But I couldn't let the men see me like this: seasoned soldiers say they can sniff fear a mile off, the way a fox smells chickens in a coop. The matter had to be dealt with without my being heavy-handed: any bias against a Volunteer would breed wholesale resentment — the opposite of camaraderie. A good session of entertainment should do the trick, I reckoned, and might give me some handle on your man. A little fun, anyway, would do us all, Volunteers of the Light-Blue Bloomer Company, a power of good.

The man to talk to was Mylie Byrne. On the night I'd been appointed captain, the men were asked to approve Byrne as my adjutant. It was more a case of reasoned judgement of the right man for the job than a return of favour for choosing me as leader. Not only did I know him, but over the previous year I'd come to learn what made Mylie tick, apart from a little weakness for the ladies — well, one lady in particular.

Mylie had this passion — no, *obsession* — for history, and got stirred up whenever the state of the country was mentioned. Sharp boys like Tommy Doran played on that. When it came to snide remarks, Doran was no way backward: an odious trait in a man carrying arms beside you. He'd try to get a rise out of Mylie over history with the intention of turning it to mockery.

The arrival of the Normans in 1169, the Penal Laws and the 1798 Rebellion were Mylie's favourites. Any remark, either, about the Act of Union, the Orange settlers who still ruled the roost in Dublin Castle, or Sir John Maxwell, who executed the 1916 leaders, was enough to get him going. Meanwhile, Tommy Doran would scan the faces of his audience, awaiting his chance to interrupt with some smart quip, and then scoff at the speaker's expense. But what Doran wouldn't spot was Byrne stopping in the middle to turn and wink. Then just before the scoffer could butt in, Byrne would change tack or ask a question, and Doran wouldn't even recognize what'd happened. Mylie Byrne had the measure of the lot of them: the actor weighing and playing to the gallery. I was glad he was on my side.

What sort of *divarsion* have you in mind? says he, when I suggested some entertainment for the men.

I'm not sure. Thought maybe you'd have some ideas.

Well, I'll tell you what'd crown the men: a few bottles of porter, a bevy of women and a good hooley, and all at once, if possible.

You mean that's what'd crown you.

You're dead right.

Fair enough so, says I.

All I had to do was contact Miss Hannah Jordan.

* * *

I had met Miss Jordan two years back, in 1917, at the Irish classes run by the Gaelic League in town. Though she was from my parish — the far end, however, and a few miles away — I'd never actually laid eyes on her till then. She even went a different road to town, herself and her friend, Miss Antwerp. So familiar was she with the town that at first I tended to be wary of her. Those who content themselves to live in towns have always a shifty bearing, with too much street savvy for their own good, which I could never quite bring myself to trust. Such enclosure, and shade from the afternoon sun, made me ill at ease. Whenever I walk on a pavement there's an insatiable urge to keep turning sideways to check my flanks, or better still to get the hell away.

Miss Jordan was a dab hand at the Irish, and because she didn't sit near the top of the class it was maybe a sign that her interest in the language was more than fanciful, not just a dip-into for the winter months. And apart from all her other more obvious . . . you know . . . female endowments, she was first and foremost a gracious lady.

She had lovely light, not quite red hair, parted off-centre, high cheekbones and a high forehead — good capacity for all that learning. You could tell by her complexion that once the summer sun came good, her face would fill with freckles. Her manner was so nymph-like that, at first glance, it made her appear smaller than she was. Such sparkle was more than bottle-fizz: her stance on the Irish language had been firmly, confidently, thought out. With poised readiness, she'd colour, rather than dominate, the debates we had when class broke up. By not foisting her opinions on everyone, she allowed those unmistakable truths of hers to be more easily absorbed and understood by the willing ear. After she had put up with the rants of opinion-gushers who might, instead of Irish, take up carpentry or lace-crochet come the next autumn, a brightness would come into Miss Jordan's blue eyes before her few short words greatly improved the discussion. Anyone whose opinions were so firmly set had to be honest and trustworthy — did it not show in those eyes? — though it was her controlled fervour that did the trick for me.

Keenness for the language was only one of her interests in the affairs of state — well, future state, for even as far back as 1917 we believed that destiny had swung our way and we'd soon have our own government. She was quick to point out how my idea of Independence, and Sinn Féin's, was simply part of a great revival then under way, which had started in the last century. While our Volunteers might gain political independence, it wouldn't mean much if we didn't revive our old traditions and language. The renewal of this ancient, noble culture would allow our nation to flower alongside the other great races of the world. That's what real independence was; it was why the Gaelic League was founded.

It was founded to spread the language, says I.

Language and independence, says she, are the outward signs of nationality.

Confuse me some more, says I.

And she laughed. The first clue, it seemed, of an understanding between us.

I found out she and her friend Miss

Antwerp were members of the town branch of Cumann na mBan. Sometimes, I'd happen on them at the fork where the two roads meet just outside town, or overtake them on the way into Irish class. Afterwards we'd chat away together as we covered the short distance back to where their road branched off.

I loved their company, the harmony between them. The two women were like sisters and seldom differed on things, except when Miss Jordan got adamant about the need for religion and priests. And not just her own: she saw value in the great world-religions; her benevolence, like her politics, was all-embracing and she appreciated the sacrifices of monks and priests. Having kept herself under duress for ages, Miss Antwerp could no longer hold back her painstaking, Protestant smirk of dissent.

While the rest of their journey was short, their safety concerned me, especially with the evenings getting dark. But they would downright refuse, to the point of annoyance, whenever I offered to travel with them. Only when the civil unrest and spate of robberies grew would they take precautions and bring Bobby Doran along. Bobby, whose brother Tommy would later join our Volunteer company, worked on the farm for Miss

Jordan's father. He was that happy-go-lucky sort you'd easily grow to like.

* * *

It wasn't until 1918 that I'd got to know Miss Jordan better. A mass gathering of Volunteers and Cumann na mBan was planned for the north of the county, over twenty miles away, to parade in protest against conscription.

Because they'd needed more soldiers to fight the Germans in the Great War, in March the British government decided to extend conscription to Ireland, but all they managed to do, however, was to cause a crisis throughout the entire country. Moderates as well as diehards were roused to rebel against such an action — heavens above, even the clergy got worked up during those last few months of the Great War. Parades and protest meetings became commonplace, and as anti-conscription fever took over you could feel the excitement, the unity of purpose, that was all around.

Our company, those who wanted to attend, were to meet outside Murphy's and cycle the road together. A small group of women turned up as well, with Miss Jordan and Miss Antwerp among them. By cycling with us, instead of the Cumann na mBan branch they were attached to in town, they were making their journey much longer for themselves.

Not travelling with the townies? I says to Miss Jordan.

We want to travel with you, says she, to help swell your ranks. The town's group is so large they won't miss a few.

Like us, they weren't wearing tunics. And it would take my brother Ben of course to pass a remark; he just couldn't bite that tongue of his.

Would it not be expected, says he, that the ladies of Cumann na mBan turn up attired in full battle regalia? For there's not in this wide world a sight more invigorating than a flock of good-looking women on the march.

I don't see you in uniform, sir, Miss Antwerp came back sharply at him. Or is this your battledress?

But Ben was no pushover. The reason we're not in uniform, miss, is because we don't have uniforms. And the reason we don't have them, miss, is because the army of the Irish Volunteers can't afford them. All items such as clothes, guns and bullets are classed as luxuries: non-essential for revolutionary undertakings. Sticks and stones are what we use in battle, mixed in with words and cants to cast spells on the enemy. Some of us might even wear kilts, miss (Mylie Byrne had let it slip that he'd like to take up Irish dancing). We might do a little jig, and put the heart crossways in our enemy at the sight of knobbly knees.

Of course, it could've been worse. Ben might've had a go at Miss Antwerp about her twang, which was very English. Or he might've gibed at her for not travelling by landau — as someone nearby had muttered — and dented the welcome given the ladies, or dampened the spirit of the sylph I had my eye on for the day. But he'd embarrassed us enough about our lack of funds: poverty was such an awkward topic among our fellows without it being made worse by the presence of women.

We had started off the day in a good mood. Maybe it was because neither Captain Nowlan nor his adjutant, Rutch Kelly, had shown up. A day spent protesting is a waste of time, Kelly had said. But since the group of women had arrived unannounced, some fellows didn't take kindly to having to mind their language, and forgo the dirty jokes too, all the way to the meeting and back.

To stub the grumpiness in time, Mylie Byrne, that man of chivalry — and opportunity — stepped forward. He made it clear that we'd be only too delighted to have the ladies of Cumann na mBan for company. Miss Jordan would feel welcome by his remarks; though I didn't know why I was so concerned about that all of a sudden.

The knight in our midst then addressed Miss Antwerp. Nothing, says he, would give me greater pleasure than the company of a lady such as yourself by my side for the journey. He even looked like an old knight as he promenaded himself over to Miss Antwerp beside her bike. It was the first I'd seen of Mylie's fad for women older than himself. Not quite fit to be his mother, Miss Antwerp was more like a mother's younger sister.

Aping Mylie, I went over to Miss Jordan, intent on escorting her for the trip, before any other brave knight bachelor might pursue the quest. How did your English friend come to be living in Ireland, says I, and become a member of a movement so firmly set against her country's occupation here?

Are you asking me if she's a spy? says Miss Jordan brusquely.

If for a moment I'd suspected her of that, do you think she'd still be alive?

Though I hadn't meant it, Miss Jordan seemed stumped by the remark.

But she regards herself as an Irish woman

now, says she. And anyway it's a long story.

Well, we have a long journey ahead, and it'll take us a while to get there.

She laughed nervously, in a way that didn't fit in with her otherwise bright, assured personality. As if in need of support, she looked across at Miss Antwerp.

Are you pair talking about me behind my back? Miss Antwerp called back. Her voice boomed out, as though she wasn't yet aware of my brother's tongue, or hadn't noticed the sniggering of the others.

We're not saying a bad word about you, says I. No sooner had I said it than I realized she didn't need my reassurance. The bond between Miss Jordan and her cut out the need for support from anyone else. This intuitive thing they had, which I'd always felt on the outside of, its strange understanding and loyalty, wouldn't tolerate the least improper remark to one regarding the other. I'd heard identical twins were like that.

Annie knows that, says Miss Jordan. She's only skitting us. Or rather, she's just skitting me; for she hasn't yet got to know you well enough to tease you. She's such great fun to be around, when you understand her.

So her name was Annie, Annie Antwerp. Let's hope Ben doesn't find that out, I thought. But before Miss Jordan could tell me more about her friend, we had to move off. The others had cycled ahead, tearing away out the far end of the village. The four of us travelled to the rear of the main group.

4

It was just as well we weren't in uniform: the Royal Irish Constabulary was out in force in each village we went through, watching us like old jackdaws on a telegraph wire. Not that it bothered us. By 1918 those boys had lost all grip on policing, the way their masters above in the Castle had lost the run of the country. Politics and democracy might've progressed over in Westminster during the nineteenth century, but the lackeys in charge in Dublin had failed to keep step.

Even more abject than their Dublin masters were these local creatures watching us, who were their bosses' eyes and ears. All information would get taken down, with pencil-stubs plucked from small black books, and wired to Dublin; then sent across to little Baby-Face in Westminster — the same geezer who wanted us to go fight his battles in the Great War. And to top it all, he would conscript us and make us fight — like hell, we would! Lloyd George and his pal King George — it was all Georges over there — could shag off, for all I cared, and fight their own Great War with the king's cousin, Kaiser Bill.

Mylie Byrne had succeeded in monopolizing Miss Antwerp's company, leaving me with Miss Jordan, which couldn't be better; it was the first time we'd been alone together. Bobby Doran, who'd been sent by Hannah's father to keep an eye on her, had got the message and cycled ahead with the main group. Except the time we came upon him, on the outskirts of the first village.

There was your man in the middle of the road, wrench in hand, bent over his back wheel. With the RIC a hundred yards or so up ahead, it was some spot to get a puncture. Or was it on purpose? Maybe he'd wanted to avoid the coppers: they might've been after him for something. And here he was taking the lie of the land.

No point in you stopping, says he; nothing you can do for me. He was too busy tapping away on the back axle to raise his head. Go on, says he; I'll catch up with you. That was the last we'd see of him for the day, I was sure.

To get us back into conversation quickly, without any awkward stillness coming between us, I asked Miss Jordan about her friend, her constant companion. I had often meant to ask before, but somehow the chance had never arisen.

Antwerp is a funny name, I said. Is it not a place in France? I must've seen it several times in snippets from newspapers, wartime reports, or heard it talked about round the fire at night.

It's in Belgium, says she. And it's not her real name; her name is Annie Martin. Of English descent, she's from South Africa originally, but when her mother died her family went to live in Antwerp. Then the war broke out, and they moved here. A neighbour of ours, who helped Annie's father unload the luggage, saw *Antwerp* stamped on a trunk tag and thought it was their surname. You know how news gets round, and so the name stuck.

When I first saw you two, I thought she was your aunt. She's much older than you, isn't she? Must be well into her thirties.

I was only trying to flatter Miss Jordan; certainly not embarrass her to such an extent she had to fall behind me on the road and hide her blushes. Anyway, it was hard to see how my words could've had that effect on her: she'd never been shy at the Irish classes. Had she grown that fond of me, she was sensitive to my compliments? Things were maybe looking up.

* * *

Chatting and getting along fine — and I'd managed not to make her self-conscious again — we were within a mile or two of the gathering when we spotted two bikes in a ditch near a field gate. Miss Antwerp and Mylie were stretched out in the field, with a carrier basket between them. The neck of a bottle lay slantwise across the basket-rim and shone in the midday April sun.

By the way Miss Antwerp was laughing, I knew Mylie was ladling on the charm he reserved especially for the ladies; he used his cache the way fishermen opened their bait-tins. Under the moustache, his teeth shone like delftware out of suds, while he gawped across into her eyes, concentrating. I'd seen fellows patiently stare over the Urrin bridge the same way, waiting for a sign of any take on their fishing lines. He didn't even bother to turn his head and acknowledge our arrival; he just casually lifted his hand and beckoned us over.

Come join us, says he. We're about to dine.

Alfresco, says Miss Antwerp. And she giggled like one half her age.

Alf who? says Mylie, still grinning and staring at her.

Miss Antwerp's giggle changed into the

deep-throated crow that'd put you in mind of the cold-start of a BSA motorbike, and her finger prodded the air for Mylie's benefit. Alfresco, says she again. It means dining out, you . . . you silly man.

Oh, does it? says he. I never knew that. Like having a picnic, is it?

Indeed, Mylie, now you've got it.

More cackling.

Miss Jordan didn't see the good of it, though, or value how well the two were getting on. She'd gone quiet, and was busying herself dismantling the basket from the carrier of her Raleigh bike, but her hands foostered too much with the cord. When I opened the gate, she marched right by me into the field and stomped past the two *cooloors* on the ground, only to stop a few yards further on. I untied my bulky gabardine coat, yanked it from the handlebars and trotted after her, like a wethersheep behind a hogget-ewe on a narrow mountain track.

By the time I caught up with Miss Jordan, she'd already begun to eat. Legs tucked under her, she sat primly on a piece of oilcloth spread over the ground. Unlike Miss Antwerp, she kept her coat and hat on, poised, ready for sudden take-off, like some wild bird at a hen's trough. Tetchiness spread out from her in hoops of iron: she held out her food, snatched at it and chewed as though it was an ordeal to eat, or at best a chore. Without raising her head, she asked if I'd care for a sandwich or a piece of cheese.

I brought my own bit, I said. Thanks. I pulled out a newspaper bundle of buttered brown-bread chunks from one pocket of my gabardine coat, and a bottle of tea from the other. There's nothing like a sup of tea for the thirst, says I. Would you like some?

She refused.

Out of devilment, I was tempted to stick the half-pint bottle under her nose; I was conscious of the holes in the wool-sock wrap, though. My bottle, anyway, was only half-full: the newspaper cork had leaked — this was always happening to me in a tear to get ready — and my topcoat was badly stained as usual.

Rowe, you'd want to get your mother to darn them socks of yours, Mylie shouted over.

Does your mother darn your clothes, too? Miss Antwerp asked him. You're no different from any other Irishman I've met: absolutely spoiled by your mother.

And have you met many other Irishmen? I says. But my question was lost.

While Miss Antwerp had been speaking, Mylie was throwing bits of grass in her face. Some went into her mouth, and she started to cough. Mylie hopped in close like a bullfrog, and rubbed her back. She was off cackling again, flicking the front of her dress. Mylie got to his feet and pulled her up.

We're going to go for a bit of a walk, says he. Me and Annie here, round the field: to shake down the grub. Aren't we, Annie?

Hannah, there's some wine left in the bottle if you'd care to indulge, Miss Antwerp called.

That's fine, Annie. I won't bother just now.

As the pair strolled towards the opposite side of the field, Mylie gave the genteel lady's rump a little nudge with his hip. Again she cackled. You never saw two characters delighting more in their roles. That long-standing drama for two, in which each allows the other's natural desires to prevail in a feast of mutual pleasure, was well under way. It would go on unchecked.

It was all very well for her, I thought. She didn't have to face old Father Cormick fulminating in the Confession box of a Saturday night. As for Mylie, he'd long before made a show of himself: giving up Confession and going to Mass. Says he: No priest is going to get his claws into me. Sinn Féin was Mylie's religion. Still and all, the clergy were four-square behind us on the issue of conscription.

Mylie's arm went round Miss Antwerp's shoulder, and rested for a while before slipping on down slowly, on the way caressing the lady's wine-coloured wool dress in puckers against her flesh. And he squeezed her round rump as though it was a sponge ball, so gently you'd hardly notice. His arm was partly covered by the coat over his shoulder — surely he wasn't expecting April showers while on retreat across the field? The picture was as potent as the luscious wine they'd quaffed, and would go to your head. At the far side, they seemed suddenly to fall through a hole in the earth. Not a sign of them, 'cept for the lady's faint English laugh.

Looking at the lone basket and the plain space the two had left, I had to shrug off a tinge of loss. I stared at the shape of the basket for a minute longer, then suddenly looked away, only to find the shape still before my eyes for a moment. The trick didn't work the second time, or the next time. Then I tried it on Miss Jordan, but it still didn't work.

Again I ran my eyes up and down the lady, stared at her outline and abruptly looked away, but I couldn't move her shape. I wouldn't have minded transferring her across the field into the long grass. I'd put my arm round her shoulder, caress her hair and hold her hand even. We'd embrace tightly for a spell, and if she were willing — only if she'd like to, mind — we'd disappear down through a hole in the field, off the face of the earth. And the hooting of two ladies, instead of one, would rise and carry across the pasture, while Ireland's cause and priests' damnations might stay on hold for an hour.

It was time for us, too, to tail-off our alfresco with some dessert. I put on a big act of reaching to grab her basket to rummage through it. This invasion of the no man's land between us would surely get her attention and provoke a reaction. Would she snatch it back, slap my hand or chide me for being nosy? Any sign, good, bad or indifferent, would be welcome. Interested in coming out to play today, little miss, out under the noon-day sun? But no, Miss J wasn't about to step out to play; no kick to her at all that day.

Take what you like, says she, drily, without as much as a glance in my direction.

I was on the point of repeating it back to her: Take what you like? Does that mean what I think it does? But such a remark at that moment would only show that I'd lost the run of myself.

I tried to figure her out. No doubt she was as browned-off in that field as a vixen in an empty hen-house, but she had only become like that since we'd caught up with the other two. Maybe their carry-on was a slight on her sense of decorum, and had embarrassed her; yet Miss Jordan had always been so level-headed. But then I thought of the identical-twins thing: the bond between the two women, its strange understanding and loyalty, which I'd always felt on the outside of. Had Annie Antwerp broken the loyalty, even violated this special liaison — whatever that might be: I didn't know their species well enough to say — and left Hannah sorely irked?

Or could it be she was just giving me the cold shoulder — some of that *Ná bac leis* we'd learned and joked about in Irish class? And the sight of the other two, cooing like a pair of birds in spring, may well have obliged her to do the same, and that frightened her off. Especially since she didn't happen to fancy enough the fellow she'd have to coo with.

She needed to have no worries on that score. I stood up and moved away from her, spread my coat on the grass, got down and stretched myself out; then I turned to face the sky and follow the moving tufts of white. The silence that'd grown between us would be used to meet my thoughts on the day's more important goings-on.

The gathering ahead would be full of flag-waving, and speechifying from the platform both widened and tapered to fit the whim of the crowd. Faces and their political parties might change, but not the reaction-rousing game of politics. I expected the new men on the scene, Roger Sweetman and James Ryan, to be the main speakers. And imagine: Sinn Féin and the clergy on the one platform. But would all their old guff amount to much, or keep us from being conscripted?

Will they be long more, I wonder? Miss Jordan says.

I'd become lackadaisical about her presence, and her voice came as an intrusion. It was time to stop lolling around.

I'm going to move on, I says. With a renewal of indifference, I stood up, got my coat, shook the grass off and slung it across my shoulder; then I picked up the half-pint bottle and flung it at the road ditch. The bottle broke into what sounded like a thousand bits: at least something was to be had by way of satisfaction. I walked out of the field and pulled the gate shut after me. The tyres hadn't lost pressure, so I lifted my bike onto the road and placed my left foot on the pedal.

Miss Jordan wasn't far behind.

★ ★ ★

Having parked our bikes inside a field on the outskirts of town, we walked a good mile to the meeting place in the church grounds. I joined the queue to add my name to the list, the Resolution against Conscription, and met Miss Jordan again under the old cross. She said she'd already added her name, when our local parish priest had organized a collection of signatures earlier in the month. So had I, but that didn't stop me signing once more.

Next thing, I spotted Rutch Kelly. The fellow who'd dismissed the notion of going there as a waste of time was wearing a hat and snazzy mackintosh like the trench coats I imagined the government spies in Dublin would have; he and Tommy Doran stood talking — why hadn't Kelly come with our group? As second in charge, in Nowlan's absence, Kelly ought to have at least told us his plans, out of courtesy if not for the sake of discipline and example. Little did we know then of the antics he could get up to.

Tommy Doran, not yet in our unit, was just home from the Great War nursing some wound or other — he didn't seem that badly injured to me. And there, not two yards from them, was his brother, Bobby; oh, he must've got his bike fixed easily, unless the village peelers had given him a hand. It was just a little unusual, though hardly alarming, to see the three of them there. But my tremor of unease was forgotten about in the middle of all that commotion.

This was a day for show, and the swagger of politicians; there was nothing that those fellows were fonder of than a chance to be seen. The bigwigs and clergy settled themselves on the stand, cleared their throats and tuned up their voices till the hullabaloo eased to a jingle-jangle. The collection of names stopped, and the first speech began.

Neither Sweetman nor Ryan was there. Instead, the big parliamentary voice of Sir Thomas Esmonde MP boomed out — 'twas easy to see the December elections were looming. Not that it mattered greatly, but I'd have liked to see Ryan, the cut of him. At least he had earned his right to pontificate, being the doctor who'd tended the wounded James Connolly in the GPO in 1916. Connolly was the leader I had most admired; the workers' man of action, and not just all words, he'd led the first Red Army in Europe — the Irish Citizen Army. Unable to stand, he had been executed while strapped to a chair; yet his sacrifice had achieved more in that final sit-down than all the Irish MPs sitting in Westminster over the previous hundred and sixteen years.

While the speeches were going on, it was Connolly's words I was thinking about: *Only the Irish working class remains as the incorruptible inheritors of the fight for freedom in Ireland*. A small farmer's son living on the side of a mountain, I was hardly the urban worker Connolly had addressed, and yet the power of his words, his dream and the action to match, cut deeper than I'd have wanted. Whereas the holding forth of well-to-do politicians — even those of Sinn Féin, who later would prove no different — could never carry the same ring of truth.

Still and all, one speaker stirred our fervour when he talked of being forced onto Flanders' fields and up the Ardennes to fight an enemy who wasn't our enemy in a cause that wasn't ours. Conscription would only add countless young Irishmen to the rotting mounds of corpses already there. As he spoke I grew more resolved than ever: if my blood was going to be spilled it would be for no cause other than the liberation of my own country.

Shouts of anger and cheers of agreement went up from the few thousand in attendance. And Miss Jordan's face was red again.

There shone in her eyes an intense

keenness and passion, a chink of which she could've done with showing earlier. She shouted, too, and looked at me strangely. And there was something else, the first time I'd noticed it all day: her scarf was mauve — yes, that was it, her favourite colour — and didn't quite match what she wore or anything else round about, 'cept maybe the colour of her rouged cheeks.

Her voice was shrill, even amid the noise of the crowd. Such an amount of passion in reaction to mere words was beyond me: women weren't going to be conscripted. If I'd made her a big speech back there in the field, would she have responded with such vigour? And, I couldn't have been mistaken here, she was excited, with a sort of zeal that would scare a body.

When the meeting ended, Volunteers and Cumann na mBan fell in, in four-deep marching formation — and in step, nearly. Miss Jordan and I found our own brigades. The parade went up to the top of the town, we fell out, then walked back to our bikes and headed for home.

The other two bikes were still at the gate, but there was neither sight nor sound of the pair — they were probably still lying in the grass at the far side. Mylie must've been speechifying something mighty. Not that I blamed him. I'd have done exactly the same, given half a chance.

* * *

The number of anti-conscription protests and meetings round the county increased through the summer of 1918, into the autumn and up to Armistice Day, in November. Miss Antwerp would travel with Mylie Byrne, while I'd end up with the other lady for company. The pair of them seldom attended a meeting, whereas she and I would turn up every time, and on time. Hell might freeze over before I'd get to lay a lusty finger on one limb of Miss Hannah Jordan, but once I'd got it straight that seducing her was beyond my ken we became companionable in a strange, even charming, way, like two maiden aunts still young enough to cycle out for a day at the seaside.

Maybe we got on more like the brother and sister whose friendship while they're growing up becomes the most trusting and confidential attachment within a family, before moving on. We two had the same dream, the one ambition, which was beyond personal gain or physical delights — mortification over pleasure, every time. And things like depending on, and looking out for, each other at meetings became second nature. And so it went, till I reached a state of mind where the thought of ever placing a hand on the lady's body was almost vile.

The friendships me and Mylie had with the two women made up for the lack of contact between our unit and Cumann na mBan; other companies in the brigade though, had long-standing links with the Women's Movement, sharing information and co-operating to tag coppers and shift weapons. The women were better at moving guns and ammunition: mettle apart, they were less likely to be accosted by the peelers. Under those big black skirts and coats they carried rifles, two at a time, from one side of town to the other in broad daylight, past the peelers patrolling the Square and streets leading off it.

I knew that should I ever need help with anything to do with furthering *the cause*, all I had to do was call on Miss Jordan. She wouldn't see us stuck — neither would Miss Antwerp.

* * *

This was my first time meeting with the lady since I'd been made captain of our company of Volunteers.

When I asked Miss Jordan if she had any

ideas about a little diversion for the lads, a party or something, it showed in her face that she was anxious to help. She would gladly have thrown a house dance or ceilidh at home herself, but her father had never taken kindly to the new republican ideal. He'd been a Redmondite, a follower of the old Parliamentary Party, and abhorred all that Gaelic revival stuff his daughter was so caught up with. So she asked me, almost pleaded, for time to come up with something.

Within a week, she was back to say that Miss Antwerp would be more than willing to hold a dance at her place, in the loft of an outhouse. The two of them would organize it, and invite a few more people along.

The lads were in the middle of drill when I gave them the news. At once their formation went awry, and the company's left-right step seemed to switch to a one, two, three. No doubt about it, it was going to be a whale of a night's session.

The promise of it did my heart good.

5

Of course, Lucy my girl, all of this happened before I met you. But when a man ages, becomes solitary and is gelded by time — with hands as clean as priests' — he is surely allowed, by way of compensation, a new freedom of speech.

I expected Sarah to be surprised, if not dismayed, at the account of my friendship with Hannah Jordan. But instead she appears more interested than ever in the story, and any time I mention either Rutch Kelly's or Miss Jordan's name her ears prick up. Indeed, something tells me there is motivation other than a hankering for history behind her desire to learn about the past. When was our daughter ever before interested in history?

If you were here, you'd tell me that the days of having to look over my shoulder are long gone — yet another benefit of ageing. Stop being suspicious of Sarah, you'd say. Trust the girl, leave her to her own devices and get on with telling her what happened. And so I shall.

⋆ ⋆ ⋆

The loft for the dance was beyond a yard at the back of Miss Antwerp's house — and what a house it was! Facing south but angled sideways, to slight even the most genteel visitor, it held definite notions of grandeur and offered a distinct snub to the likes of us. The way it stood haughtily alone from its surroundings, this bald-faced entity looked for — no, demanded — notice. At the same time it didn't need to have an attitude befitting some puffed-up middle-class monstrosity you'd see on the outskirts of town; it was, after all, quite a pleasing mound of masonry.

So pleasing, you couldn't help but let your eye rest on those good looks. Low rooflines lay in gentle contrast to gable verticals, but enough space, if only just, allowed for the eaves-overhang to be sharply trimmed by a neat fascia — such a delicate border between wall and roof. But that wasn't what really held the eye. Its splendour was, as with all beautiful things, more inbuilt, and took time to grasp, then appreciated, before being finally admired.

That was it, the relationships were right: the overall height as against the overall width — one, probably, an exact multiple of the other — or where some other formula for classic proportion had been used. If only I could've held my thumb steady before my eye for long enough to measure. And from where we were, it had the correct width to match its length. A lawn, though not very well kept, ran all round it. Without outhouses or trees immediately nearby, it stood alone in its own space.

Is there anything the matter with your thumb? says Mylie Byrne. You're doing great looking at it.

Off to one side, a few outhouses showed through the trees, but once the spring got going and the foliage came on full, they'd no longer be visible. Then it hit me. What gave this place its real majesty was a feature more hidden even than its proportion. The final, distinctive mark of pedigree to the property was bestowed by what came to within a field or two of the rear.

The mighty woods of old Killoughrim were the true taste of heritage there, and added a beauty to the house that surpassed the man-made or any contrivance of finery. In times gone by, this strange forest had covered a full barony, nourished an ancient people and sheltered rapparees and villains down the years. Many an oak beam in a London mansion was purloined from there, leaving the earth scarred and raw — but ripe and rich for Cromwell's hoors of landlords. So the ancient people had no choice but to withdraw to the sides of those blue-black hills, or *beyant*, west, to the bogs of Connacht.

In our early youth, myself and Mylie Byrne had followed the river Urrin down to the forest after trout and salmon — the few that would make it there from the sea. There was surely no better spot to dodge the river bailiff. We'd always keep a few paces between us: if your man were to nab one of us, the other could sneak up behind and give him a clout on the head — for all bailiffs should be able to swim.

Man and daughter, so, could hardly ask for finer heritage on their doorstep, or a better spot to live. And wasn't it great for the Antwerps to be able to look out on this scene every morning — and well they might afford it: having arrived there by way of South Africa and then Belgium. Anyway, who'd begrudge it to them? They were a decent enough family.

It was a little outrageous then, no doubt, that a band of rebels should put a foot on their property, let alone be invited up to the house. But this is how it was. The owners were English — African- or Belgian-English: no matter which — while we were dedicated to casting off their country's grip on us. And yet here we were sauntering up the avenue, on our way to a party being thrown on our behalf. It made no earthly sense; it ran against the grain, but was all the more pleasurable for that.

★ ★ ★

For a laugh, the way children would, myself and Mylie trudged through the round pebbles of the driveway, a driveway that curved too much — overly la-di-da for the size of the two-storey building it led to.

A low one-bar metal railing, on thinly spaced uprights, ran along either side of the drive, and splayed off round the house to meet again at the back, probably (who could be bothered to find out?). The thing was so slight it hardly had a purpose, and Mylie demonstrated this when he stood way back, hands on hips, letting on to be a high-jumper; he ran and made a great hop across the railing. Hurrah, says he, as if he'd won first prize at an athletics meet. And the lads behind shouted and clapped.

It turned out to be a three-storey house after all; the sudden basin-like dip in which it stood meant that the basement couldn't be seen till we were close up.

So this is where the in-laws live, says I.

If they're my in-laws, I'm their outlaw, says Mylie.

Where'll it be tonight for you, Mylie Byrne, I ribbed. On the long grass at the far end of yon field or on the chaste lounge in the drawing room? You can't meet your father-in-law looking like that. Here, let me fix your quiff. And I spat on my hand and made a shape to reach his head.

Get away, you dirty article, and keep your black paws to yourself. He said it in that casual way of his, not the least perturbed, bent sideways and brushed away my hand.

Just at that moment a piano sounded through the partially raised bottom sash of a great window to the left — one of only four windows at the front, apart from those in the basement — the drawing room, probably. Somebody inside was showing off, judging by the speed of fingers up and down the keyboard scales. Then came the first bars of a tune, and a voice broke into song. It was a man's voice, rich and strong, not quite a tenor's — maybe a tenor, I wasn't sure — and we had to stop and listen.

She is far from the land where her
young hero sleeps,
And lovers are round her sighing;

But coldly she turns from their gaze,
and weeps,
For her heart in his grave is lying!

She sings the wild songs of her dear
native plains,
Every note which he loved awaking;
Ah! little they think who delight in her
strains,
How the heart of the minstrel is break-
ing!

By then there were six or seven of us outside listening: the lads behind had caught up. When I asked who the singer was, Tommy Doran said it was Rutch Kelly.

No! Mylie refused to believe him, saying that Kelly was far too ignorant to be able to sing like that.

Ben Rowe told us all to shut up and listen as the singing continued.

He had lived for his love, for his coun-
try he died,
They were all that to life had entwined
him;
Nor soon shall the tears of his country
be dried,
Nor long will his love stay behind him.

Oh! Make her a grave where the sun-
beams rest,
When they promise a glorious morrow;
They'll shine o'er her sleep, like a smile
from the west,
From her own loved island of sorrow!

The big voice inside had finished and, as expected, was about to start the first verse again. Without need of invitation, we looked at one another, nodded to count down the beats and, at the top of our voices, launched into this external chorus — heedless of keeping in time with the tenor inside.

She is far from the land . . .

Miss Antwerp came to the window, raised the sash higher and leaned out on the sill. She had a special grin for Mylie, secret from all the lads. Well, nearly all — just as well, for his sake, my brother Ben hadn't yet found out about them. It was hard to spot, knowing Mylie, but I thought something showed in his face. The music and singing inside stopped in deference to our arrival.

We kept the song going, thumped our chests, went down on one knee and, with outstretched arms, made a meal of it; in mockery not just of the performance inside, but also the outrageous notion that one of our fellows could engage in such grandiosity that was a cut or two above his station. Then for no reason other than out of respect for the patriot whom the song was about, the outside chorus became in deadly earnest with its singing. We still couldn't match the voice inside; for all that, our feel for the words was no less valid.

She is far from the land . . .

The front door clunked, the weatherboard dragged an arc along the floor back into a vast hall and Hannah Jordan appeared, nymph-like and lovelier than ever. Again I felt the same old rush at seeing her, quenched almost at once by a dearth of anything to look forward to, only want of hope, and more damned mortification over pleasure. She turned, and we crossed the walkway to follow her into the hall.

You could fit the whole of your house in this space alone and bring your mother and brother, I said to Mylie. You'll make a grand knight of this castle. When we come to rob, you can pull up the drawbridge to keep us out.

But Mylie only turned his head and flashed the crockery at me in mock contempt.

Before us, the great stairs and its balustrading, centred between the walls of the stairwell, rose to a half-landing and then divided in two the rest of the way up: the shape of a mighty bird of prey about to land — surely not a phoenix? The notion of flight also came from two carved eagle heads where the handrails ended at the ground-floor newels. The builder had made certain the visitor wouldn't miss his stairs anyway, or his idea of majestic flight. Your man Pugin, who'd designed the big church in town, would've had to stop to gaze in admiration.

But against all this, time, as measured in years of decay, and human neglect and abandonment, had united here to oppose the builder's idea of splendid order. Many of the black and white floor tiles were cracked, and paint flaked wholesale off the skirting onto the floor. Patches in the carpet running narrow-cut up the stairs were so threadbare the canvas fibres lay unravelled amid dust and fluff-balls on every step. Such an age, too, since the stair rods had been cleaned, it was impossible to tell if they were brass.

Barely inside the front door, we were, when Mylie started sniffing, craned his neck and raised an eye to the ceiling. He gave me a nudge to look.

I don't like the ears on that boy up there,

he said. A mushroom was growing in the middle of a large brown stain in one corner under the stair landing. They'll have a job getting rid of that, says he. Mylie knew a little about these things: when he was younger, he'd worked with his father, a mason.

You'll have your work cut out here, says I.

But again he flashed the teeth. And we followed Hannah Jordan into the room.

⋆ ⋆ ⋆

With one elbow resting on top of the upright piano, Rutch Kelly had made himself at home; he had more right to be there, his stance said, than anyone else. His chin never once lifted to greet us; instead he stood twiddling one of the black-japanned candle-holders with his other hand.

Hey, Rutch, says Mylie. Mind you don't pull that curlicue off the piano there; them's delicate features, you know.

Sure you'll be able to fix it if he breaks it, Mylie, I said.

Kelly blushed a little, more from rising anger, you can be sure, than loss of face, and at not being able to react there the way he knew best. His nose had been put out of joint by our arrival, and the pride of place his voice had won him was under threat. He had to be admired, though, for being sharp enough to get there and establish himself before the rest of us. Did he know the people of the house? I had a mind to pick up on Mylie's remarks, and make Kelly more uncomfortable; to take him down a peg or two more.

But that's not what the evening was about. We had to keep in mind why we were there in the first place and not spoil everything. Some decorum was called for; so before anyone else got a chance, I bellowed out my tuppence worth.

When I was outside, there was glorious singing going on in here. And I'd love to hear it again. Whose voice was it? Let's hear it.

Yes, of course, Richard dear, says Miss Antwerp. Please do. Rend our heartstrings with yet another of your exquisite *chansons*. At once.

I loved the way that woman put things. Mylie and herself were a perfect match, but for the age difference. Poor *Richard dear* blushed a little more, and I knew he'd sing again; wouldn't be able to stop himself. My brother stood just inside the door: ears cocked, eyes moving and eyebrows a-twitch, but if he too was out of his depth he didn't let it be seen.

Is it dear Myles, or Myles dear, we are to address you from now on? I asked him beside me. Have you got your 'Shaw's song' ready? You're next up to sing.

Now that Miss Antwerp wore flat shoes, her ankles showed that she was no spring chicken — though, according to my mother, it was the neck that gave away a woman's age. Inclined towards stockiness, like the rest of her, they were also slightly out of plumb, and her feet splayed outwards.

When it came to looks, the shape of an ankle settled it for me: whether a girl was lovely or just plain. A dainty ankle always held the promise of more delicacies, mainly hidden ones — that subtle beauty thing again, like proportion. I just loved to gorge my eyes on good ankle curves, to let them rest there a while, the way you'd slowly suck a September pear — before dinner. Another advantage of ankle-gazing: you might stare at them for ever without being called a gawk. *Oh, he's a very shy boy: he keeps looking at the floor all the time. Pity about the beak on his face*.

Hannah Jordan had her usual ankle-high boots on that evening, and I was still without an exact measure of those lower joints — or any other joint, for that matter. If her visible curves, though, were anything to go by, the others were bound to be pleasing. She'd already taken her place at the piano to accompany the singer — so it was she we'd heard from outside. Full of surprises, she was.

Here was another fine room: a deal wider than the hall but not as deep, and the ceiling was lower, perhaps because of the stairs in the other room. It was a good deal less tatty, with skirting and cornices to match those of the hall. With shapes mirrored and lines continued throughout, the house's pattern of unbroken design carried inside from without — or was it the other way round? Surely, there was no place more fitting for the repeated notes of piano and fine vocal strains to rise and harmonize.

At the side of the piano, Rutch Kelly straightened himself up, stuck out his chest and waited for the first few introductory bars before bursting into another exquisite *chanson*:

Believe me, if all those endearing young
charms,
Which I gaze on so fondly to-day . . .

Not another one of Moore's blooming melodies! Did the man know nothing else? I sidled over to old greybeard in the armchair to see what sort of codger Miss Antwerp had for a father, assuming he was her father. He sat with his arms resting on his knees so that both sets of limbs doddered away together there nice and evenly, but despite the shakes and his frame having seen better days, he was a jaunty devil. He sat up straight, ready to let anyone know that he wasn't the least impressed with what his senses were telling him. And a sharp enough old boy he was too, having spotted not only my sudden lack of interest in Kelly's singing, but my manner and gait since I'd come into the room.

Are you the top cat among these vagabonds my daughter has got herself mixed up with? says he. Might I be so bold as to suggest you watch your back when dealing with the warbler there? Age teaches you about men, and I recognize a parvenu when I see one: he will climb your back to reach the sweetie jar.

And I'd thought his daughter had a way of putting things!

To show that I could look out for myself, I was tempted to retaliate: It's not Rutch Kelly you need to concern yourself with, bossman, but that rogue Mylie Byrne, who's wangling such hot, fond affection from your darling, chunky daughter. I caught myself in time: such a remark would've hardly been apt.

May I suggest something else? says he. Do not leave your aft-deck exposed to a certain harpy among the unwholesome companions my daughter has thought fit to surround herself with.

Miss Antwerp came over, bent towards her father and, finger to her lips, shushed him. She turned to me, caught my arm and led me through an opening at the end of the room. She closed the door behind us and nudged her back against it till the lock clicked home.

The evening light was gone, or the little that was left couldn't find its way through the window of the study at the back of the house. This room being only a third the size of the other, prominent things looked massive in the half-dark. Bookshelves on two walls rose all the way to the ceiling, and between them stood a great desk with an inlaid black-leather top surrounded by mahogany, or walnut — Mylie Byrne could tell by just a feel. Why was I thinking of him again? A couch stretched before the window — more black leather — with space enough behind for someone to lie in wait. It was a soldier's duty to remain alert, I reminded myself, and a captain's to be ever watchful of his flanks.

Any big house like this might have a shotgun put by in a corner, rather than hung over the mantelpiece. Would a fellow be ever so lucky as to get his hands on a rifle? For a moment there, I'd forgotten that the lady of the house was one of us. I felt out of my depth and twitchy. My head swivelled too much, like an RIC man's on duty at a Fair Day. But that was nothing to the sensation of what followed.

My jawbone felt so sharp against her palms. Her fingers were soft and warm; their sudden heat to my body settled any fretfulness, and fixed all curiosity in one direction — japers, woman, what are you doing to me? Miss Antwerp's hands moved about my face, while she hushed me the way she'd hushed her father earlier.

I'm confused, says I. What are we doing here? Your father and I were only having a quiet chat — he is your father, isn't he? We didn't talk out loud, or interrupt the performance. Do you want to see me about something, in private?

I'll tell you what I want, says she, ignoring the question about her father. And the next minute her hands were around my neck. A pleasant slow-falling feeling suffused my brain. The most luscious, warm, moist lips I'd ever tasted were suddenly glued to mine. Her body pressed hard, with an intensity that might be deemed untoward. She pulled back her mouth for an instant, only for an instant, and said: Shh . . . Let's not interrupt the performance. Her wants had become clear — heavens above, but she was the lively beast of a woman.

The singer, now on his second time round on that song, belted out his words of caution: *As the sun-flower turns to her god, when he sets, / The same look which she turn'd, when he rose*. Caution be damned!

During the next few minutes all resistance, training and curiosity about guns faded. This soldier, like many another, broke rank and closed down signal lines to HQ upstairs in his head, and instead took orders from a different quarter, that outpost of rebel command which had suddenly become too prominent round the nether regions — *forward, quick march*! Anarchy was setting in.

Let's go somewhere more private, she whispered.

Oh, such sweet words! If she'd added *my dear* to them, they might've been from a melody — and hardly one of Moore's either. The sheer luxury of her *more private* brought on a sweet loss of memory, as you'd feel while downing a few balls of malt after drill, of a night's hoar frost, amid the promise of yet more warm joys and ecstasy.

But as applause for Rutch Kelly resounded, good old HQ reopened signal lines. I was picturing Mylie Byrne's face again. Anarchy had to be put down. I pulled back from Miss Antwerp, held her at arm's length and made the excuse of having to hurry out and meet the others from our company so they'd know where to go on arrival.

Ah well, she sighed. It was quite delicious while it lasted, don't you agree? We must pick up on this again, when you become less tense. But you need not worry about the evening's arrangements. Come along and I'll show you.

She linked her arm with mine and led me into the hall, then through a narrow passage at the back of the house, where she collected a hurricane lamp, and out into a small yard. We went along a narrow path through an area of coarse grass, and into the farmyard whose out-houses at the far end I'd spotted earlier through the trees. Up a set of stone steps to a corn loft, she lifted the latch and opened the door.

The large space was lit by a number of wall lamps turned up to the full. A group of men, probably the musicians, were standing round, drinking bottles of beer or porter. One fellow, who wasn't drinking, sat and tapped impatiently on a kettledrum. When the men saw us, they collected their bottles, went over to their instruments and began arranging them: ready to play, but awaiting the go-ahead.

Nobody has arrived yet, says Miss Antwerp. She waved to the men, turned on her heels and we two went outside. Careful down the steps, says she. At the bottom, she linked arms again, and marched us over to an arched opening into the barn below the loft. She handed me the hurricane, went ahead inside and lit a wall lamp. At first a glow spread in a patch across the yard, but as more lamps were lit the glow increased to a decent brightness.

I went back as far as the house with Miss Antwerp, handed her the lamp and turned to stay outside. She refused the lamp: You hold on to it till the others arrive.

She went inside and, within minutes, one light after the other flickered in all the windows, till the building became like a business house in town of a Christmas Eve. Relieved to be alone, out by the edge of darkness, I then felt a shiver of pleasure just to look in at such brightness, and more than ten years fell away. I almost expected to hear the ring of shop-tills again, or feel the touch of my father's hand pull the rug over me and my mother in the tub-trap, as he tried to keep her sweet lest she scowled on getting the whiff of spirits on his breath. A clack to the pony, and we'd head up into the dark beyond town.

Soft rain began to fall, and I turned my head upwards. Nothing in the world can quite match the caress of rain from the south on your face, as it skews its way from Ross and the coast. For a moment or two, I felt perfectly free, unfettered.

As the men arrived, walking over the gravel, I directed them past the house and up to the loft, till our company to a man had turned up. Right away, they got stuck in: bottle after bottle from the stacked wooden crates, tomfooling about while awaiting the others from the house. The musicians started, but it wasn't until the women of Cumann na mBan and their friends from town arrived that the dancing got going, and increased till the floor shook like it might collapse.

Sorely tempted, I was, to forget my role and join in as the tempo rose. There were too many dangers, though, if everything were left to the vagaries of night. I had no choice in the matter: a watch would have to be kept. So I stood out on the steps, or walked up and down the entrance drive and path from the house, while, inside, jigs and reels rose to fever pitch, and men drank their fill.

And Mylie Byrne's wish had come about: the porter, the bevy of women and a good hooley, and all at once. Nothing was impossible any more.

6

But, something else took place that night. At the time the chance meeting didn't amount to much, or come like a flash of lightning to burst open the night sky. It was a case of two people, strangers at sea in the world, bumping into each other, that's all.

Among the women who'd cycled out from town for the ceilidh was this attractive, not overly gorgeous or strikingly pretty, young one who possessed a certain delicate charm. Her face and trim dark figure appealed to me, but there was nothing more about her than could easily be overlooked amid the other chocolate-box glamour girls. Mind you, she had a fine clump of black curls you wouldn't forget: from low on her forehead, the mane tumbled in disarray to her shoulders.

By heavens, that she was whirling on the arm of Rutch Kelly was enough to wet my whistle. He could dance too, the hoor, as well as sing. Having a right little chat with him, she had a lovely smile as she lapped up his old *plausy*. Was he trying to get places with her? Like bloody hell! Obstacles were going to be put in his way. Aside from seeing him galled, there was a more delicate reason, though this was no more yet than a fleck in an amethyst, maybe, of future chance.

It was hardly the first time that I'd been wrenched between the goings-on inside and my duty to keep watch. The men's welfare, however, had prevailed over each temptation. But this was too much: I had to step in and join the dance. I waited till opportunity came my way, when Kelly went over to one of his pals — probably to boast about how well he was doing with the women.

Where had the mysterious girl gone? Ah yes, there she was near the door, waving her friend's cigarette smoke from her face. Not used to cigarettes, her friend puffed like a single-stroke engine. A pair of gaunt fingers held the dirty rotten thing too close for comfort before putting it back between their owner's lips. I'd once heard Miss Antwerp call a girl *a puffing ingénue*; at last I knew what it meant. I'd been to the Saltee Islands once, and seen the red-billed puffins of early summer. Your one, too, had a mighty red beak on her.

I felt my neck throb and my knees wobble unsteadily. I made it to where she was standing, and paused for a moment to gather myself. Then, will you dance with me? says I.

I felt rather than saw two pairs of eyes look

me up and down. Afraid it hadn't been made plain which one I'd asked, I stared at the dark-haired girl and ignored the other, the puffin.

I will and all, she chirped, merry as a bird — glad to be getting away from the chimney facing her. She smiled and followed me onto the floor. There was something lovely about her smile that I hadn't expected, a smile to melt gems with. And she carried herself so very well, too.

How do you put up with the smoke? says I.

She didn't answer, only smiled again, though not as much as before — a touch aloof?

Although the loft-boards weren't quite up to it for dancing, we managed to waltz fairly well together. My right hand felt her firm waist, while my left held her right hand; she was no bother to lead, turn and swing about. I even chanced a fancy curlicue with her at the corners — a risk I seldom took with a partner on the first waltz.

You're a topping dancer, says I. And again she let go with her full smile: lovely — a fellow couldn't ask for more than to see this girl beam.

After that waltz, another and yet another. I wanted to dance with her all night. But I was neglecting my job; so I explained myself and reluctantly took my leave. Our meeting had amounted to more than just a few dances. And what Rutch Kelly might do after that, or however much he might chase her, no longer concerned me: I had a sense that I'd just raised the fence too high for him to cross. Her smile stayed with me going outside, and lit the night dark.

At the same time I was wary: town girls lived too close to the side of the street to be entirely trustworthy. And for a young one, she could dance too well. But her smile was so beguiling it would belie all experience and build-up of secrets that survival on the streets demanded. Neah, even if she knew more than she was letting on, did it matter? I walked up and down the main entrance a few times, then went back to ask her for another waltz. But she'd gone.

Looking for that old thing I saw you dancing with earlier? says Mylie — the fox had come from nowhere to nudge me in the back. She's gone back to the house with a group of girls, says he. But you wouldn't want to let the grass grow under your feet: I saw Rutch Kelly throwing the eye over her, feeling for child-bearing hips and checking her fingers to see could they milk a cow. I'm off now to look for the queer one. Do you want me to pass on a message? She might come out to the back door to give you a goodnight peck on the cheek.

Leave her alone, says I.

Mylie went out, down the loft steps and off in the direction of the main house.

Miss Antwerp let the girls stay in the house overnight, under the guise of being there on bivouac, or some other exercise — Cumann na mBan's assignments, no less than our own, were ever secret. And I'd had to give Miss Antwerp an assurance that any man staying the night would confine himself to the loft or outhouses, and no shenanigans.

I was more concerned about keeping a look-out for the RIC, in case the local coppers had got wind of our shindig and decided to pay us a visit — informers were everywhere. From the middle of the previous year, 1918, any gathering of more than ten people was an offence.

By half past three in the morning, the musicians had packed away their instruments and headed off, and an hour later I was able to snuff out the lamps. I did a quick head count of the lads: half of them had gone home, and the rest lay snoring across bundles of corn sacks at the far end of the loft. Rutch Kelly was among them, snorting like a horse — a relief. Asleep or awake, the man sang.

I was about to snuff out the last wick when

Hannah Jordan appeared and picked up a few bottles that were strewn about. She asked me if I wanted to go back to the house for a cup of tea and a bite to eat: our first words since we'd arrived; I'd hardly laid eyes on her more than once in between.

Yes, surely, after I've gone down and put out the lamps underneath.

Come on so, and I'll help you, says she.

I didn't see you out dancing at all.

No, I was inside keeping an eye on the house.

I'd hoped to have a dance with you, says I.

We pulled the loft door on the snoring, and went down the steps. Below, one or two of the lamps had already burned out for want of paraffin, while the others, in less draughty positions, had a little oil left. We walked past a few farm carts whose shafts rested on the ground; unused in years, they looked slightly forlorn. The last one had its shafts raised in the air, having been left upended after its load had slid half-off, the hay still sitting over its back rim, as if somebody'd had to rush away. Then I noticed a rag on the end of one of the shafts. But no, not a rag at all, it was a pair of blue bloomers — a pity they weren't black: they might've belonged to Maud Gonne. I reached up, plucked them off, and was surprised at how warm the material felt. Tired of all decorum, I waved them full sail in front of Miss Jordan.

Whose item of clothing is this? says I.

Not mine, says she crossly. By way of subtle distraction, she turned her eyes to the ground, picked up another beer bottle and emptied the dregs.

I couldn't mistake the same old manner of remove again. No doubt I'd behaved in an unbecoming way, worse than raucous even, but I was too tired to give a damn. The quicker we finished, had that cup of tea and a bite to eat, the sooner I could get back for a wink of sleep — that load of hay by the upturned cart looked a comfortable enough spot.

I jumped when a woman's voice called out.

At your convenience, James, would you pass me the garment you now hold in your hand? I do believe it's mine, Miss Antwerp said. Yes, it has to be mine, though I'm not quite sure where I put it. She popped her head from behind the load of hay.

No, James, you never managed the impossible. To remove the same said article — oh, thank you, James! — off our dear Hannah here, alas, would prove to be beyond even your resourcefulness.

Her expression changed. The self-satisfied touch of fun disappeared, and in its place was a look of horror: her jaw dropped, an open-fingered hand held her mouth before it could fall any further, and she inhaled with the awe of seeing a ghost.

Oh, James, you mean you don't know? My innocent boy, I am so sorry. An oversight on my part, I assure you. But did you not even suspect? And to have left you two together: it must've been a terrible tease. Simply gauche of me. But I had thought, dear boy, that you were aware all along, such composure and serene acceptance you showed. And what a trick of fate: you appeared to be the most soulful, compatible chums. Please, do forgive my not recognizing the love interest on your part, James. I really should've guessed. I do hope Hannah hasn't become your heart's desire . . . Oh James, your heart isn't broken, is it? You are certain, though, the thought never once crossed your mind — you had not even the slightest inkling? Oh, well! I consider it incumbent upon me to remove you from your ignorance at once. Let me see, how might I put this . . .

I'm afraid our dear Hannah inveterately and incorrigibly finds solace and delight only within the lay of a lady's placket. Quite unlike myself in this respect: I relish my cornucopia where I find it, as you may have guessed. She shows not the least proclivity towards the male equivalent, the codpiece, you understand. Codpiece or placket, whichever: it's all the same to me. I will not make flesh of one and fish of another . . . Haw, my little joke, you see.

And, dear James, had you but known this earlier tonight, you might have had your passions pleasured, instead of saving yourself in vain. I'm afraid, however, you've missed your chance — missed mine too. You've been too tardy again. For at this hour I am a deal overworked and greatly overspent. Isn't that so, Myles, you naughty boy? But we really must do something to sort you out, James, after all your hard work and patience, your dedication to the cause.

Mylie's head appeared, ever so gently raising itself alongside hers. He had the look of a sheep, and appeared to be as confounded as I was. He slowly turned his head from me to Miss Antwerp and back again. Though he did so a few times, this didn't ease his confusion one iota. But finally a hint of the old grin broke out on his face.

I think I know what she means, says he, through the teeth.

You can tell me again sometime, says I, turning to walk away.

The final stillness of late night had settled over everything as Miss Jordan kept pace with me across the farmyard and we made our way along the narrow path towards the house, where the lights still shone from the windows like it was Christmas in the town. Maybe that was why I was happy to be going in there again out of the dark.

7

We have so many things to go back over, Lucy Brien, and, if you were around, this would be a two-way conversation — you were hardly short of an opinion, ever. You remember the night: the dance in Miss Antwerp's loft? Again and again, I picture you waving the cigarette smoke from your young face.

What's this, it was about you? Ah, that smile, if I recall rightly: as instant and bright as sunlight through rain, and it got me from the start. Between a hint of a smirk, questioning any matter that was less than wholesome — balderdash, you called it — and a fully fledged beam that bespoke only pure delight, there were at least a thousand variations; any one of them used to light the night dark, and still does, more than ever. You remember how we waltzed? *Dededa, dededa, dededee dededom* . . .

Before that, I'd caught a glimpse of you dancing with Rutch Kelly. The very thought of your hair and soft skin coming within range of his lascivious claw puts such a rage in my gut that I want to go find and geld the crab, this instant.

Since then, prickly flashes of the way you two moved on the floor have come back to mar the picture. But such questions — too invasive and abject for a decent man to ask his wife — would've led to a breach of trust. However, since you're no longer with us, I can allow myself to pose them. The picture hinted at a touch of complicity . . . Well, was there some little thing going on between the pair of you? Surely not. A lady like you would never have allowed herself to entertain the least interest in him. Though when they heard him sing, the girls could be taken in — a temporary lapse, forgetful of the fiend behind the voice.

From that night on, I kept an eye out, but it was a long while before we met again. You remember it, don't you? That stretch in the infirmary, when we could meet freely and spend hours together: the getting-to-know-you part of our lives. A time of charm.

* * *

No, we didn't meet again till the summer of '22, early on in the Civil War that followed the Tan War. I'd been wounded and taken to the infirmary; the enemy would soon come after me. When the bullet was removed, two of the nurses, who were members of Cumann na mBan, moved me to a safe place, a quiet storeroom full of spare beds, and screened me off in a corner with mattresses stacked on end.

Was I surprised to see you? I hadn't known you worked there, though Mylie Byrne had told me you were a nurse. That fellow must've known of every pretty girl in the county! The sight of your face trebled my rate of recovery, but I couldn't let on or I'd've been given short shrift from there. Whenever your roster changed — remember how you tried to explain it, while I kept interrupting? — you couldn't get to look in on me so often. It was all talk between us for a while, till that time I couldn't resist you any longer. I reached out, put my arm about your waist, and asked if yours was going to be an arranged marriage too.

You said sharply: That's only for farmers' sons and daughters — people who marry for land and convenience. Townspeople marry for love.

So they make their own arrangements?

Yes.

In that case so, says I, I'd be glad of your hand in marriage.

But you're not a townie, you said, testing if I was in earnest.

So townies have a monopoly on love? says I. Must be the narrow streets, the lack of space between the houses and all that close-up living.

The surprise you got could hardly hide the smile, or the *tocht* in your voice. My arm moved further up your body and tested for resistance; when there was none, I had to pull you into the bed beside me. The touch of teasing was immediately swept aside by passion of the most ferocious kind.

It was outside all laws of decency, or how I'd otherwise have wished things to be: from the moment you relented to my touch, I had no doubt but you were saying yes to my proposal. More than that even: the bond of matrimony actually came into being there and then — I felt it; saw it in your manner. A wonderful, permanent and safe world was made, in which only me and you existed as its centre. Neither ring nor rite was needed to make a marriage: our fervour was contract enough. That was our first honeymoon night.

Over the next few weeks, the passion was wholesale; fervour was turned into a vehement thing and made irreversible this side of death. Pure delight, that first honeymoon — for wasn't that what it was, without the unveiling as such? Tell me you don't remember the evening; you thought you'd locked the door, and in came that crotchety old nun, Sister Concepta, to find the two of us threshing away beneath the blankets. I was the one to emerge from underneath.

Mr Rowe, says she in disgust. Is that a girl you have there in the bed? Is it not enough that we offer you sanctuary, but you must turn round and abuse our generosity by bringing in your whores, turning the infirmary into a brothel?

Mind your tongue, Sister. I'll have you know this girl is no whore; she's my wife. And you happen to be interrupting a man and woman carrying out the duties assigned them by nature and the contract of marriage — the sacrament of the church. You have your vocation and I have mine. So I'd appreciate your removing yourself and your vocation to let me get on with mine. And at once.

The old girl turned, swished her black and white habit like a hooded crow after a shower, and blustered out of the room, sternly chanting her Latin office: *Coitus interruptus, glory be, coitus interruptus . . .*

Just as well you kept your head under the blanket, and that she didn't spot your uniform, or, Lucy Brien, you'd've been out on your ear. Ah, but I never got round to telling you — so many things I've wanted to tell you — once the uniform was removed from your pure white body, I always made sure to throw the bedspread across it — just in case, force of habit: keeping an eye on the flanks, you see.

Though we were married, we didn't go through the ritual of nuptials for another ten years, and only a handful of people knew. It was what you wanted: to finish your training, and get in a bit of nursing. I'd have preferred otherwise. I have often suspected that you were loath to come live with me on the mountain, and it was hard to blame you: no comparison could be made between the life of a nurse surrounded by town comforts and the hardship of a sheep farmer's wife. Of course when you eventually moved, you transformed the house — and did so without raising the hackles of the old pair. My mother and father, by then growing feeble, took to you from the beginning, and everything went well.

They were the good years. First of all you brought two fine sons into the world, and in the year '41, during the Emergency — with the world again at war, a time of ration books and scarcity — Sarah arrived. But those years passed all too quickly.

Your face changed. I first noticed it about two years before the end, but said nothing — didn't know what to say to you. There was a look of wax about your temples, cheeks and under your eyes — in the eye itself, the iris yellowed, the pupil dulled — and a ghastly whiff of *keenagh-lee* on your breath. I knew the signs all right. If I could've turned back the clock, I'd have left you in town, kept things the way they'd been. I might have you with me yet. A precious few years indeed: from the early delights through to watching you fade, and then the final decline, those last few days. And all I could do was watch.

You blamed the infirmary: something you picked up while working there — we'll never know. Neither priest nor doctor was of much use anyway. By the middle of September 1950, you were gone . . .

September's a peculiar month. It was the coldest autumn day, and a wind cut down through Scullogue Gap. It nipped at our ankles, or so they said — I couldn't tell: standing in the graveyard, there was nothing but cold in my bones. And I've not properly warmed up since. You lie there in the one plot with the old pair, above on the side of the hill, for ever a mountain woman now, and with room beside you for one more.

8

Throughout 1919 and 1920, our company continued to march and drill, expecting that soon we'd get the order for an all-out strike against British forces. To begin with in the campaign, we'd jab the underbelly of the monster with hit-and-run tactics and ambushes, like the Munster men were doing, tactics the Boers had used in Africa. And by the end of 1920 anyway, such fighting was well under way in Munster and Dublin. It was a matter of patience; all we needed were munitions, and the order.

One of these days, I was sure, a boat would dock and we'd get word to head for Waterford or the port of Ross, to collect our allocation. Hadn't Commander-in-Chief Collins sent our former brigade CO to America for guns? He'd been ordered to go quietly lest news got back to informers. Local gossip had it that the man had scarpered — though we, to whom it mattered most, knew better. But as 1920 came to a close with still no sign of guns, we grew discontented. With nothing in sight, drill became tedious and spirits ebbed.

It was two years since Armistice Day and

the threat of conscription had come and gone; with no immediate urgency looming, our numbers had dropped. To make it worse, regular word came of how the Munster brigades were doing. Even the Dublin men were back in the fray, after the flop of the Easter Rising not five years previous, and Connolly's Citizen Army was still going strong. If only the man himself had been there to lead us!

And though we got word our new CO was trying to source weapons through his contacts in France and that plans were afoot for an intensive-training camp for a whole new active-service unit, it was hard to understand our brigade's inaction. Jerry Tobin thought our CO needed more time, despite the fact that it was the previous year that Collins had ordered each brigade to have its own Flying Column. So why couldn't we be given the go-ahead to do something in the meantime? Anything to let loose on those blackguards, the Black and Tans, who'd been in our country since March 1920, and to pay them back for murdering our people, destroying homes and looting.

Sent here by Lloyd George's Coalition Cabinet to augment the Irish police, which had become a fairly demoralized lot, most of this new force had been recruited from demobbed troops who'd been idle since the Great War, and were, without the proper training, more familiar with trench warfare than with the duties of policing. Attracted to the job only by the promised sum of ten shillings a week, each recruit was handed an odd combination of dark-green tunic, khaki trousers and black belt to wear. They turned out to be an undisciplined mob of neither police nor soldiers, and were soon nick-named, after a well-known Limerick pack of hunting dogs, the Black and Tans. The Tans patrolled our land and struck terror into every village and house.

Throughout the latter part of 1920, the Tans had scoured the countryside, stopping their lorries to shoot people at will. In the next parish, and on the same morning, two young men, brothers, and a middle-aged man were shot and bayoneted to death by His Majesty's special recruits.

Like every other brigade company, we received a master plan — more paper: no shortage of that from HQ — giving us our course of action in the event of an all-out strike, when the order to attack would come through the local post office. Its details were to be kept secret even from our men; only the captain and his adjutant would know them. Possession of the document alone amounted to a serious crime, under Regulation 18 of the Defence of the Realm Act, if you don't mind.

First, we'd attack and seize the local RIC barracks, capture and hold the coppers in the one cell; then take all post offices within our area. We'd open up at least two lines of communication: one with battalion HQ and the other with brigade HQ. Strict military law would be enforced, and our proclamations — *Looters and persons suspected of giving information to the enemy*, etc. — posted up in public places. At least the confidentiality surrounding the plan showed us we were part of a national scheme of things, if a general Rising, like that of 1916, should break out. This master plan, however, was the only meaningful set of instructions we received at that time: we heard nothing about a strategy for immediate action nor a word about guns.

By January 1921, martial law had been extended to our county of Wexford. Then one night in late February, a few miles from home, the enemy burned down Mrs Murphy's and Peig Cuffe's private school, the Irish school. The only warning given was a revolver thrust through a window, and a voice calling on the women to get out.

Early the following morning, Mylie Byrne called at my house with the news. On his way out the yard, he turned and said: Let's do something.

⋆ ⋆ ⋆

I knew I'd have to sound out the lads before taking any action not ordered by HQ, so the next evening after drill I asked a small number of old stalwarts to meet me in the back bar of Murphy's. The meeting was restricted to the trusted few among us, and the order given: strictly no mention outside of anything discussed — and each man was made to swear to it. There were reasons for this.

Something had bothered me over the previous few months, I wasn't sure what. It was more of a shadow than anything definite: a forewarning, like a carrion crow hovering. You'd notice little things: a lorry mooching along the other side of the valley — more than once. The engine whine, carried away by the evening breeze, would fade altogether when the machine halted behind a clump of trees. Then a flash of brilliance like the glint of a star at night: the lens of a telescope or field glasses? I mentioned it only to Mylie Byrne and my brother Ben.

We varied training locations, yet there were still signs: a movement on the horizon, the shape that seemed to slip behind a tree trunk, but nothing more of note than a fleck caught in the corner of my eye. Yet, wherever we'd set up, there was always some portent or glimpse of a phantom, or *thivish*.

Soon suspicion grew to a strong sense of disquiet: not only were the peelers aware of us, they had details of training and names as well. So had England's greatest ally, and curse of every rebellion for seven hundred years, come back to haunt us? Was there an informer in our area?

* * *

Mylie Byrne, Tommy Doran, Jerry Tobin, myself and Ben sat hunched round a table in Murphy's. Even though the Great War had ended more than two years previous, Lord Kitchener's massive Kerry finger still pointed from the wall poster above us, doing his job, recruiting away for himself. His face reminded me of one ruddy gob a lot closer to home and every bit as much in need of a good belt. But Kitchener's *boodhawn* didn't bother us, so long as it didn't have ears. Instead, we used him to order drink.

Hey, barman, this is your commander-in-chief here, Kitchener of Khartoum — K of K. I'm pointing at you. *Your king and country need you*: fill up our glasses once more.

And I'm pointing back at you, old Murphy would shout. You're barred from these premises.

Bar me from this pub tonight, my old *segotia*, and tomorrow morning you'll have no pub to run. We'll scorch the locks of your bald head, and the black clinkers of Kitchener's *gowlogue* into the bargain, if you don't fill us up and be quick about it.

Even though a picture of the monarch was hanging inside the front door, that too was all right: we knew the true lie of Murphy's loyalties. Sympathies rather than symbols would carry the day. We understood the fine line he had to walk along to stay open. From any one of four roads, troop lorries might appear within minutes at the cross, and pull up at this watering hole. While we scarpered out the back, Murphy would have to stay, and together with the troops, old Kitchener and the monarch, they could all have a right royal old time of it.

At least you fellows buy your drinks, old Murphy had said. Your enemies drink their fill and then stick revolvers in our faces when we look for payment.

We chatted about the burning of the Irish school, news of the Tans' other exploits and the exasperation of not being able to strike back. Then it was time to face the reason for the meeting. I broached the subject from a particular angle: as if we'd already discussed this matter, that there was no need to cover old ground about the decision reached and I was taking it for granted that an ambush on the Tans was definitely going ahead.

We'll have to pick the right spot, says I.

The eyes of all four faces immediately stared at me. There was no humming and hawing any more, or shades of grey: the moment had come to stand to either one side or the other of the line. There was a long thick quiet. It wasn't till I noticed the familiar twitch to Mylie Byrne's mouth, as if he were thinking of some plump older woman, that I knew it was all right to continue with this.

We'll have to rely on shotguns, since there's no sign of rifles. So the spot we pick must allow us to work at close quarters, and we'll bring knives, just in case, for finishing-off.

Have you got approval? says Ben.

Our approval comes from the need to stop the Sassenachs doing what they like and moving freely in these parts. If that means going against the wishes of the brass in town, then so be it. I'm prepared to stand over an order.

There'll be no consequences to giving such an order, I suppose? says Ben. You won't be disciplined or court-martialled? And I suppose we won't have Tans by the lorryload, knocking on every door between here and Vinegar Hill, to wreak havoc. And do you not reckon that, while we take to the hills, those left behind will suffer reprisal for us? The ordinary people will surely thank you for bringing all that on their heads.

When the brother bites, caustic soda would be mild in comparison. But I was used to his tongue, which seldom spoke less than the truth. I'd learned long before that the only way to handle Ben was to spoon him a dose of his own medicine.

So do you want us to go along with the brigade brass in town: keep on speechifying, and doing nothing? Or maybe that's why you joined the Volunteers in the first place: to do nothing? If you're so afraid of what's ahead, this is your chance now to bale out.

Don't get tetchy, says he. I'm not disagreeing with you; only pointing out the consequences a Volunteer worth his salt ought to think about.

So there under the picture of old Lord Kitch it was agreed to answer Mylie Byrne's call to do something. But before carrying out any attack, we'd need guns. And it was up to me to figure out a way to get our hands on them.

9

A dog was barking, the sound intensifying till the animal's full-blown loathing echoed sharply across the yard behind the house.

We watched in the dark as the light in a room went out and the window shutters were closed. Then one by one, steadily but quickly, the remaining downstairs lights died, the way the candles at midnight Mass are snuffed out — such a full-bodied smell of hot wax to top up the darkness and heavy pall left over from Good Friday. For a moment, I could almost get the whiff of candles again, and feel regret that a certain something was missing.

If there's a smell in heaven, it must surely be that ripe mix of candle grease and incense you get at Easter ceremonies. Strange, how notions from nowhere suddenly catch up with you at the right-wrong moment. I'd get back, though, I promised myself, on the straight and narrow: back to church of a Sunday and Saturday-night confession — you'd feel so *spanty* new coming out — when all this trouble would end. But I couldn't chance it just yet — couldn't risk being excommunicated. The clergy never took kindly to rebels, and only the few good ones stuck with the people even in '98. Yet we never felt more in need of a minister than when we were in the black business of fighting.

During the Troubles the fear never left me that I might not get a decent burial in the event of being shot; that no priest would stand over my remains with the rites, and give me the password to go and join the old stock — those who'd carried the bloodline down the ages. I'd not get to stand in the valley beyond the mountain with the old warriors of my tribe, proud of my attempts, adding to theirs, to free our race from tyranny. I feared being left to rot in some ditch, with no one to give out the word — that franchised formula spoken over the dead. No hope for my *thivish* then, but to flap the air over Colclough's fields for all time, like a swan from the story of Lir.

As the lights in the windows ahead went out and downstairs the house got dark, my fear worsened till anguish set in. More and more I craved that whiff of candles and incense again, because they were forever linked to light and hope.

* * *

Would the upstairs windows get blanked out too? In these troubled times, surely two women who lived alone would expect something like this. At least they'd got a warning. The one thing I hadn't allowed for was that damned dog barking: my lack of experience in this business showed. I'd been so sure — though sureness was a dangerous trait in soldiers — that we would surprise the occupants and get in there easily. But my plan had been scuppered, and by a fecking dog.

The occupants of the house would surely go upstairs and board themselves into one room, and if we were, say, to put a ladder against the wall they'd close all upstairs windows, except to the room where they had retreated. That way, we would know exactly where they were. And if one of us rattled the ladder to distract them, the main raiding party could go round and force the back door and get inside without being fired on.

Tommy Doran had suggested getting some child from the locality — where had I heard that before? — or even an adult, to go knock on the front door. Recognizing the caller, the old ladies would surely open up, and we could appear from nowhere to pounce. But I'd decided it was too risky to involve anyone other than the women indoors.

Ben whispered: If there's a gun in the

house, the chances are it's already loaded and one of them is now on her way upstairs, and about to point it through a first-floor window. So let's watch for any movement up there.

As far as we could see, the three upstairs windows at the front were open. And it seemed our best means of getting inside might be through one of them, if only a ladder could be quickly placed against the wall beneath. I'd already sent Mylie Byrne to look for a ladder in the yard, but he was taking an age to return.

You slip around the back, says I to Tommy Doran, and examine the windows, upstairs and down, and tell that other lazy lout to hurry on with a ladder.

* * *

It made sense for a unit to raid for arms well away from its own area, where, no matter how good the disguise, you would be recognized. Is it you, Jim Rowe? someone would say. What are you doing with that thing on your head? I'd know that gait of yours anywhere. I see you're still wearing those old trousers your cousin sent you from America.

Instead, Volunteers would pass on information — about gentry and big houses likely to have shotguns — to a company from another area. It was normal enough so for a unit to travel long distances on raids, and without having to bother with disguise.

One of Tommy Doran's cousins from the third battalion had told him about this place. Two ladies were running a school here for butter-making and poultry-rearing, and they kept a pair of shotguns, which they'd refused to hand over to the police for safekeeping. It was hard to blame them: to be left on their own, unarmed and in the countryside during a time of trouble, meant their house was easy prey to every common thief. By holding on to their guns, however, the women were tempting an altogether different fate.

At intervals and in pairs, we'd arrived well before dusk and left our bikes in a field down the road, with Mylie Byrne's younger brother, Will, posted there to mind them. All fourteen of us had then slipped along at intervals under cover of the roadside hedges till we reached the field adjoining the buildings.

I'd given them their instructions for the raid. To keep the number entering the house to a minimum, three fellows would stand guard to the front, and three off to the rear. Mylie Byrne would search for a ladder. In the meantime Tommy Doran and I would make a wide sweep round the premises, before settling on where we'd go in. But then the dog started up, and the more we moved the more he barked, till he reached his crescendo.

Within a few minutes a head appeared at an upstairs window, and the top sash opened down further. The person there lingered a while, watching. We at once knew the location of one woman, and if we could only look closer we'd surely spot the barrel of a gun jutting out. But was the second woman there with her? We'd have to wait and see.

Next the shutters of a downstairs window were pulled back. The bottom sash was forced up ever so slowly, and I could make out the upper half of a man's body with arms resting on the sill. By heavens, we hadn't been told of a man being about the place. Was there more than one: a blooming troop maybe? Were we expected? Had someone informed? Then one arm began waving frantically.

Mylie Byrne must've forced his way in through the back door or found an open window. It wasn't what I'd ordered him to do, but no matter: we'd made an entrance. But whereabouts was that second woman? I circled round by the side of the house, then over to the front, where Mylie was waiting, hands still resting on the sill.

What's keeping you? says he, in a low voice. He was as casual as you like, as if this had been the plan all along and the rest of us had slipped up. Come on, will you, says he; I left the back door open. Only, mind the buckets in the scullery. 'Tis harder behind there to get through than for a poor man to grope a duchess in the dark.

You'd know all about that, Mylie, says I.

I gave the others the beck to follow, and we made our way round the back and sidled in the door. We felt each step past the buckets on the scullery floor, past the pots and pans, through the kitchen to the hall leading to the front and into the room where I'd seen Mylie. It was much warmer there, 'cept for the breeze from the front window. The smell, so different from the smack of carbolic acid we'd met in the scullery, was of smoke — a nice fire was glowing in the grate. This must be their living room.

Right, says I, anxious to get a handle on the situation again, and miffed at Mylie's waywardness. First thing, let's put our hands on those two women.

There was a snigger in the dark. They're too old for that, came a voice.

We mustn't let them out of the house till we've finished the job.

Another guffaw. I could allow for such nervousness.

Now they've probably got a shotgun

apiece, so be careful, I told them. Or the laugh will be on the other side of your face. One more thing: if there's a complaint afterwards of anything been lifted — money, jewellery, whatever the item — the culprit will be court-martialled back in the judge's house. Not so much as a hair of the women's heads will a finger be laid to either. Understand?

I realized then I should've called an inspection back in the field, and grilled the company: 'twas the only way to keep manners on those fellows. That's what would happen before the next operation.

Five of us did a quick once-over of the ground floor and returned to the room, where Mylie again stood looking out the window, hands propped on the sill like he was used to the place. Squire Byrne. He then suddenly closed the window and made for the room door.

I'll go up first, says Squire Byrne. I know how to climb wooden stairs without making a noise. Wait there by the door till I call you from the landing above, and then come after me the way I'll show you.

Going up the stairs Mylie spread his weight on his hands and feet, like an infant. Each step was taken by gently placing hands and feet as close as possible to the strings of the stairs, as if he were treading on coals. The squire had become a circus monkey. Almost at the half-landing, he was, when one step made a loud creak. The noise alerted someone above, and there was a slip-slap of feet crossing the floor-boards of the room over our heads.

Mylie came flying down the stairs the opposite of the way he went up — an antelope rather than a macaque monkey — as if he expected some safari hunter in khakis to tear after him. We all took on a fleeing state of mind, and hid behind the open door of the room. Mylie came in and ran over to the window. There were other footsteps coming down the stairs: probably one of the women. Mylie had time — only just — to lift the bottom sash again and pike-dive out underneath, like he was throwing himself into the river Urrin for a dip after a hot summer's day slaving in the mill.

A blast went off with a flash like lightning that lit the room for a long moment. My eardrums felt deafened. It was more like the nerve-shattering boom of some old howitzer than a shotgun going off. Burnt powder infused the air, and we drew all of it in, it seemed, through our nostrils. The frilled valance of the curtain fell down slantwise in puckers across the window.

I wasn't worried about lead shot hitting

Mylie: I knew he'd got out in time. But the blast had shattered the glass in the window, and sent the shards flying after him, from which he'd hardly have had time to escape.

Before the safari hunter could even think of firing the second barrel, two of the men nabbed the woman at the door, took the gun and dragged her into the room. Ben closed the door firmly, and kept his fist tight round the white enamel knob. I lit one of the oil lamps over the fireplace, screwed down the wick, put the globe back on and waited a minute or two for the glass to warm, before turning the flame up to the full. Then I told Ben and another fellow to light all the lamps downstairs.

It was time to deal with the old tartar, so we sat her down for a chat. Even in daylight, 'twould have been hard to put an age on her other than she was well over forty and as grey as a badger. Gradually, Parnell's big bearded parliamentary head looked down askance at us from the painting over the mantel — no question about the political allegiance of this house.

Who else is here? I barked. We intend you no harm, and have not come for your money; nor will we take anything other than what you should've already handed over to the peelers. We're not common thieves, you know. Guns are what we want: all that you have. So please co-operate with us, or else we'll tear the house apart till we find them. Do yourself a favour and save trouble by handing them over at once. But first, who else is here, and where are they?

The grey-haired lady wouldn't open her mouth. So, as gently as possible, we raised her from the chair, bound her hands and marched her in front of us up the stairs. Having warned the second woman to come out quietly, we stood the first one at the door of the only room not yet checked, and waited. Don't shoot, I called, or you'll hit this woman. After a few minutes without a response, I asked the lady to tell her companion to come out.

Come on, Alice, she called. Give them the gun. There's no point in making it worse. They'll only tear down the house on us.

The door slowly opened, and the second lady peered out and handed over her shotgun. The worst was over. The next thing was to search for cartridges and more guns.

Go downstairs, I said to Ben, and look for a crowbar and some tools. We'll just have to rip the place apart.

That won't be necessary, says Alice — exactly what I hoped she'd say. We'll give you what we have. She led us into a small inner room on the ground floor, probably a study, unlocked a heavy door and then opened a pair of panel doors to a secluded cabinet-rack. We could hardly believe our luck. Sweet Alice above!

This particular raid gave us our best haul by far. Seven shotguns — well, six, to be exact: one was an old musket of a thing, which we left behind — and a few dozen cartridges, though afterwards I had an idea that we'd missed out on boxes of cartridges. We bundled up our take under the hallway lamp: the guns in three separate jute sacks, and we wrapped the ammunition in two oilcloth carrier bags we'd found in a drawer in the kitchen to hold it dry. I decided to leave the women in the sitting room, having warned them not to venture out till exactly one hour after our departure. A few more jobs like this, I thought, and we could launch our first attack.

But in all the fuss we'd forgotten about Mylie's posterior when he'd dived out of the window. Ready for the road, we were, when the front door opened and in he comes, hobbling like a cripple. His hands were all bloody. It wasn't till then that I realized someone should've checked up on him.

Were yous going to leave me out there to bleed to death? says Mylie. And me opening up the place, so you could walk in the door like gentry attending a ball.

Why didn't you go out to the boys on watch and keep them informed about what was happening? I told him. I had to say something not to let him think he'd been abandoned.

For all they know we might be dead by this stage, says I. We've finished now and are ready to go. Are you all right there?

For all anyone knows *I* might be dead, says he. And then he slowly turned round, like he was in a passion play. The seat of his trousers, what was left of it, was torn and red and the cut flesh of his posterior showed as he leaned forward for us to have a good look. There was only one thing to do.

Come on, says I. And I went over, grabbed him from behind and lifted him clean off the floor. I called to one of the lads to nab his feet. We carried him into the kitchen, laid him face down on the table and pulled his pants down round his ankles. I went into the other room for the two women — who no doubt had hoped they'd seen the end of us. At first they were most reluctant to lift a finger to help, but when they saw Mylie stretched and bleeding on their table they took to cleaning him up like they were nurses in the county infirmary.

The red soap was found, then a press by itself high on the wall was opened and bits and bobs taken down. They picked his bare backside for splinters and washed him, while I held a lamp close by. Not since he was an infant did Mylie's rear end get such a going over. He turned his head to me and winced.

Stay quiet and don't break wind, says I, or you'll be in worse trouble.

It was the wrong thing to say, and Alice and the other woman stared at me, then dabbed Mylie with cotton wool for another five minutes, as though his buttocks were being pickled for posterity and locked away inside a jar on a larder shelf beside the preserved onions and beetroot. What was this fascination women, young and old, seemed to have with Mylie's rear end? Even when that delicate business was over, the pair of sadists wouldn't let go of him. Out came the iodine bottle and a crow's feather.

Now we'd see Mylie pout. At the first touch of the feather, his chin drops, his mouth opens and his lips curl inwards like a toothless old fellow whose face is prevented from being sucked in any further by round-topped gums.

They went at Mylie with the venom of jilted wives who'd just found a chance for atonement; those two women made him pay for the night's violation of their home. The first to fall victim, Mylie's rump was their pound of flesh. The pair of hussies even exchanged a quick smile as the iodine turned yellow on his skin.

Ben gave a shout: Will you look at his big yellow *tóin*? Do you never wipe that thing, Mylie?

And he could do with a good shave too, someone else quipped.

This remark seemed to be the last straw, as far as the women's patience with us was concerned, and they stepped back in disgust from the table. Without as much as another word, they'd finished. One of them poured water into an enamel basin from a galvanized bucket, while the other scrubbed her hands, scrubbed and scrubbed again. I'm glad I never married a man, said Alice.

Am I ready for the road? Mylie enquired, as if asking leave to go home. And when the nurses didn't acknowledge him, he levered himself off the table, still making faces. Would someone be so kind as to pull up my britches for me — what's left of them? But nobody would, we could only laugh. Ah, come on, says he. Though, when one of the women turned to come over, he put up his hand and said: No, no, it's all right. I can manage on my own.

Eventually we thanked the women and set off, Mylie hanging on to Ben and me as we made our way down the road towards the bikes. On the downhill parts of the road, he tried to ride his bike standing up, while the rest of us took ourselves home. All in all, it had been a good night's work.

* * *

Our next raid was on the nearest RIC barracks, at a crossroads a few miles away. Like most other small outlying barracks as the Troubles worsened, the peelers there would withdraw to the nearest town before dark every evening.

But they didn't leave the place an easy target for the likes of us. It must've taken them half the day to open the barracks, and the other half to turn it into a fortress again. With so many locks on doors and window-barricades, they hardly had time to write up their little black books. Every possible entrance was so well secured that it would've taken us too long to break them in, never mind the risk of drawing attention from the local copper-fearing lackeys.

It was a job for the ladder again. We took to the back roof to remove a yard or so of slates high up; then, as Jerry Tobin shaded the hurricane lamp with his coat, in we went under the rafters, and down through the lattice-and-plaster ceiling. Along with a window in each wall overlooking the cross-roads, the corner office upstairs, probably the sergeant's, had a tall steel cabinet heavily fixed to the floor and bolted to the wall. But Tommy Doran was able to open the front panel. There were only three rifles, a Webley revolver and a Mills grenade inside, but, no matter: every little helped.

A heavy safe stood firm against an outside wall. There was no point bothering with that thing, I allowed: not enough time, and the force would've blown the safe clean through the wall, onto the road below — and sent neighbours reaching for their blinds and window lace.

Before going down the stairs, I had a quick look round. I saw nothing much, except a large brown envelope, hardly noticeable, pinned between the leg of a chair and the safe. It must've slipped from a tray the sergeant was putting into the safe last thing that evening. Inside a second envelope within was a handwritten list of all the men in our company, and my name was at the top of that list. I stuffed it inside my topcoat and made my way downstairs.

Halfway down, I heard one of the lads

shout: Stand back! So we took cover as there followed a small blast to let us out the front door — Tommy Doran was a dab hand with explosives — and we were away. The peelers would find an extra few things to do the next morning.

* * *

Over the following weeks, we carried out more raids on farmhouses, all well outside our own area, of course, and picked up more shotguns and boxes of cartridges. Some of the men, the farmers among us, brought shotguns of their own.

At last we were ready for some action.

10

I have sharp memories not only of what was done to people's property but also of what was done to people themselves. Many of the actions we took were, to say the least, unbecoming — maybe profane is the apt word. What makes this story so difficult to relate — and no longer is it enough to *think* about the particulars, it seems, I must now recount them as well — is the fact that I was the one who gave the orders to have these things carried out. And till the day he dies, each captain carries the evidence of his orders not as stripes on his shoulders but as marks across his soul.

Though you may've heard snippets of such deeds from other sources — the local gossipers, mind you, have yet to face me with their accursed rumours — I could never bring myself to tell you the full story, Lucy Brien. I didn't want to bother you with the leavings of my guilt: a man ought to pay the price of his actions without whingeing on anyone else's shoulder; and to become a toady and look for a woman's sympathy was hardly a trait you'd have liked either in a man. And it's easier, too, to control memories by not discussing them — not even with you. Besides, there was an accord, understood between old comrades and rivals alike, that when it came to the subject of the Troubles we would always keep our tongues tied.

With the insight of age, though, I sometimes have second thoughts about the benefits of such secrecy. Apart from the right of access the next generation has to history, it goes against his nature for a man to impose a lifetime of silence on matters that affect him greatly. Indeed, nowadays it's almost the fashion for people to unburden their guilt by talking about it.

But is it not a bit much to expect an old man, fifty years on, to overhaul his long-standing taste for silence? Like every soldier must for the rest of his life, I've successfully managed to regard — no, to dismiss — those more unpleasant aspects of our company's engagements as all part of war, the throes necessarily involved in achieving the birth of liberation for a land. And despite any regrets, I still firmly believe that every order and action was justified and carried out only with the best interests of my country at heart. So regrets and second thoughts be damned; I can ill afford to indulge in such blether.

I know what you'd say to me now, loud and

clear: For heaven's sake, what's the fuss? Get on and tell our daughter what happened. She has a right to know.

And since she's heard so much already, I suppose I can hardly be accused of breaking the code of silence by telling Sarah the story in full — if only the telling of what happened were all there was to it.

⋆ ⋆ ⋆

It was the final week of February 1921. Though a fortnight had passed since the last snowfall, a few shiny half-crowns persisted to hold on to their ground where the sun couldn't reach.

For some time myself and Mylie Byrne had been scouting the main road out from town, to establish the pattern of the journeys the Tans made on this route. One spot in particular gripped our attention: further down, the Cutting Road, built during the Famine, where my grandfather — an old man in the corner by the time I knew him — had worked, breaking stones. Hungry men had picked their way there through solid rock, nearly twenty feet deep in parts of this three-hundred-yard stretch, leaving sheer walls on either side, like a small gorge. This same spot might yet be remembered in song and story as the Gorge of Retribution. Besides being suitable for an ambush, there seemed to me to be no more fitting a place to exact restitution.

If we thought things out carefully and planned properly, I believed we could waylay an even more wanton villain than the one who'd forced starvation on our ancestors. The desire to send the guilty straight to hell where they belonged, alongside their brethren of yore who'd tramped the old road, burned every church in sight and worn red coats instead of dark green, was like a hunger in my gut. The Tans, too, had raided and destroyed homes. Would we never see the end of their likes: hoors' spawn, every last one of them, since that first great hoor, Strongbow, stepped off his high prow in 1170 and looked round, licking his fat greedy lips.

This stretch of ground had been violated ever since. But by all that was sacred, I swore we'd make a stand on this patch of stone, and fall down dead defending it, rather than let those violators have a free hand to carry out their reign of terror much longer.

⋆ ⋆ ⋆

Every weekday morning, two Tan lorries drove out on the road from town and passed this spot between ten and half past — and never ran late. But their return in the evening was less punctual. As we crouched and hid in the previous year's growth over the road, we'd watch their faces: the driver and the two scoundrels in the front beside him in each lorry. We could pick out the whites of their eyes through the wood and brass spyglass lent to us. I felt a tic in my lower eyelid when their alien faces neared and, twenty yards apart, they drove right under our noses. As they passed, we'd look into the trailer behind with the canvas flaps tied up, where members of the main group sat facing each other, chatting and nodding to the movement of the lorry. They always seemed more at ease on the return trip.

Evening after evening, we watched their return. We got to know their faces: the drivers' and those who sat up front beside them. We even put names on them, dogs' names: Shep, Rover, Little Fido, Mangy Matt and Black Bob. For a lark, we called the drivers after two women: Horny Han always drove in front of Angel Annie. Indeed, they looked almost human, and not at all like the subspecies between man and ape as shown in their behaviour. Altogether the two lorries carried no more than fifteen of the enemy.

Within a few miles of their barracks and

with heads nodding, those fellows were ready to fall asleep: satisfied after their day's outing of hunt and pillage, and much less alert than in the morning. No doubt about it, the enemy was ready for waylaying on their return journey. A good evening's duck shoot it was going to be for sixteen or seventeen men of our company. Then, after that, we'd have the whole night ahead to cover our tracks, without fear of pursuit from enemy search parties.

First and foremost, we'd have to work out details and prepare ourselves for every eventuality. The men needed drilling and a few days' intensive training immediately before the engagement. The spirit of a piker, that real meanness, would have to be instilled. As things stood, their frame of mind wasn't ready for the job of killing. Tommy Doran, a man who'd already tasted blood while out foreign in the British Army, pointed this out to me — his experience was becoming ever more valuable. But could Rutch Kelly and Jerry Tobin, or anybody else for that matter, including myself, be relied upon in a close encounter? We'd soon find out. Come hell or high water, this job was going to get done.

Like a tradesman needs tools, we'd have to become better equipped. Because of our positions, directly above the enemy, grenades would be our main weapons. We'd need at least twenty of the Mills type, and mines too — more than just the one we had found in the raid on the barracks — and some ammo for the three rifles to pick off those who'd escape the main grenade onslaught.

We thought the other two local companies might lend us rifles, but not the rounds: lack of ammunition had already restricted their activities. The problem with telling their captains anything was that they'd want to send along some of their Volunteers — men we wouldn't know well enough and who'd end up causing more trouble than their worth. And since we were going ahead, anyway, without approval from brigade HQ in town, we didn't want truck with anyone else. The only outside help we were willing to accept was from Cumann na mBan.

The next evening Mylie and I were kicking through the stones along the drive to Miss Antwerp's big house once more. I had to tell Hannah Jordan about our plans for the attack, the weapons we needed and when we'd want them.

Though she couldn't say for sure that she'd procure the necessary guns, she would of course do her best for us. She told me she had contacts high up in the women's organization, which would have the wherewithal to acquire what we needed. She warned me, though, to be very discreet about our arrangement; if word should get back to her immediate superiors, they'd surely accuse her of exceeding her authority by going over their heads.

Since we were going to push ahead without approval from our brigade, I asked her in turn not to spill the beans or say which company the stuff was for.

Or the town leaders will court-martial you, says she.

They wouldn't dare, says I. Court-martial us for attacking a few Tans, who are harassing our families? Indeed, our action may have the opposite effect on the brigade: shame them into sorting out their squabbles and doing something useful.

They'll still reprimand you for not getting approval, says she.

Not at all. Now, how soon can you tell us about the stuff we need?

Hannah Jordan didn't answer me. Instead she went on about the bigger picture: our ancient culture, what it means to be Irish and, her favourite subject, of course, the language. Oh no, not again, I thought.

But the lady could do more than talk. A few days later, I got word to call at Miss

Antwerp's house to meet Miss Jordan. Wasn't it a bit peculiar, though, that she should see fit to use her friend's home in all her dealings with us, as if we were to be kept at arm's length? She'd mentioned that her father, an old Redmondite, was none too pleased about her involvement in the new nationalist movement. Politics, he believed, not virulence and violence, was the way to manage business with Westminster. Nothing would ever be achieved through aggression, except bloodshed, martial law and restriction — like what was then being imposed on us. But his crowd had seen their day, as was evident in the previous election when they were almost wiped out.

Hannah Jordan said: You'll find the items you requested at the railway station in town in four days' time, at six o'clock in the evening. A number of packages will be addressed to you personally.

At last we were going to be up and running.

* * *

With such wet during the first few days of March, the last coins of snow quickly vanished — March many weathers, they say. A breeze swept down the Cutting Road as would snap the beak off a *Goureen-roe*. I couldn't tell whether I was shaking from cold or from nerves about what lay ahead. I could've done with Mylie Byrne beside me at that moment; his easygoing assurances would've been most welcome. Instead he was across from me on the other side of the gorge.

We'd managed to assemble twenty Volunteers for this operation, and I felt strangely vulnerable with only three of them alongside me in my group. For the formation of this ambush, I had divided the men into four groups and staggered them on either side of the gorge so that the operation extended over a distance of no more than fifty yards. The second section of four, under Tommy Doran's command, was positioned forty yards further on towards town, on my side of the road. Mylie Byrne was in charge of the section not quite opposite me, about eight yards further back towards the mountain. The fourth section was on Mylie Byrne's side of the road, again about eight yards back from being opposite to Tommy Doran. I gave Rutch Kelly charge of that lot. Two unarmed men were posted on the road back towards the mountain. The nearest would give us the beck when he'd got a signal from the other — on a bend a hundred yards further away — that the lorries were coming. The third look-out was posted down the road on the town side of our location, as a precaution more than anything else.

We were ready for them. The road had been holed in two spots the night before, then refilled; so all we'd had to do was scrape out the holes quickly, place and cover the mines and hide the wires. After letting the first lorry pass, I would blow the second lorry the instant its front axle was over the mine, and Tommy Doran, located slightly back from his section, would blow the first. Then we'd hit them with grenades, which we expected would complete the job, with little need to use the shotguns. We'd managed to get four rifles, which we'd given to the four best target men — one with each section — so if any Tan escaped beyond range of the shotguns he'd get picked off by rifle.

Across the way, Mylie pointed to let me know he was checking his watch — again. The lorries were already ten minutes behind time. Unusual: the Tans had never been this late returning to base. They had to have been delayed: a wheel frame damaged, an engine breakdown or something; maybe the bastards had ventured too far into the next county and got waylaid back there — those scallion-eaters were no joke when they got going. More likely, though, the Tans had been extra busy that day, rampaging and bayoneting information out of those not quick-witted enough to keep out of their way.

Another ten minutes passed with still no signal from the look-outs. There was a red light flashing in my head. Had anybody given the game away? Maybe one of the lads had let word slip, and the wrong person had got wind of it?

We waited till after nightfall, when it was too dark — even had the lorries come — to do the job, then I blew the whistle and we disbanded. Myself and Tommy Doran disconnected and removed the mines.

⋆ ⋆ ⋆

Afterwards, I questioned each of the lads about where he'd been and with whom he'd been talking, even in passing, since I'd told them about the upcoming attack. And had he told anyone in his family, even though he'd been warned, again and again, not to breathe a word?

I put Mylie Byrne through the same grilling — no exceptions — and asked him if he'd said anything to Miss Antwerp. He then turned and quizzed me. I must admit I was a little taken aback, but it made me check on those I'd had dealings with. The only people, it seemed, who knew about the operation were the men of the company, Hannah Jordan and a few women from Cumann na mBan who were in on the supply of arms.

Miss Jordan didn't seem pleased to be questioned, though I explained the situation and told her that everyone, including myself, was being grilled. Her demeanour didn't change and she was still loath to answer any question. I was surprised by her snooty reaction; she'd always been so willing to assist us.

However, someone must've let it slip, and for days and nights afterwards I picked it to pieces in my head.

If the Tans had expected an attack, said Tommy Doran, they'd have stopped the lorries away up the road, come round our flanks and finished us off. How the hell would he know what the Tans might do? He'd served as a regular in the British Army; whereas the Tans were neither police nor regular troops.

It was hard to trust anyone any more. But one thing was certain: while this might have been our first attempt, it certainly wasn't going to be our last. We'd keep up the momentum, once we'd got things going, procured a few more rifles and explosives through Hannah Jordan, as well as a shotgun apiece.

For the next few mornings and evenings, myself and Mylie returned to the same spot to observe. The lorries didn't show at all the following day, but they were back on schedule again the day after that. We moved with the greatest possible stealth, in case we were being watched.

By heaven, the next ambush would be different, I decided. As few people as possible would know of our plans, and I warned the men: any evening, instead of drill, the company might mobilize for action again and, after an engagement with enemy forces, would remain together till the following day, or even longer. *Be prepared* was the motto.

Each time there was drill, every Volunteer was to bring what food he needed and the minimum gear for one night's bivouac — an oilcloth groundsheet and two blankets. And every soldier was reminded to keep his gun as good as new. For at last we were carrying a shotgun apiece instead of the old mock-up.

11

No, a fellow didn't have to stop and pinch himself. The time had come when a Volunteer could carry a gun round with him without the least compunction that he might be breaking the law.

The idea had turned to reality: we were on the brink of a new age. Though more than two years had passed since the 1918 General Election, followed by the setting up of Dáil Éireann, our Parliament's Lower House, the allegiance due to Government was beginning to have an enriched meaning for each Volunteer. We were in the throes of forging our new nation, and rebels no longer needed to skulk along by the other side of a road ditch, for we'd become soldiers in the army of the Irish Republic — the Irish Republican Army. And an IRA man's greatest role now was to uphold the new legitimate authority that'd given us this status. A man could stick out his chest and raise his head.

Of course, our new system's roots would be well tested before the enemy would let go and acknowledge its right to exist. But the soldier of the Republic was proud to put his back to the wheel. Where his loyalty lay was never to be doubted again, and he'd fight to keep his nation and government in place. This showed in the approach of each man to his unit. It knocked jizz into his marching step, though it didn't affect diehards such as Mylie Byrne, who'd always believed in the justification of armed struggle.

But, Mylie, violence is wrong, an old Parliamentary Party supporter in Murphy's had insisted.

How do you get back what's been taken from you? Mylie replied. Go plead with your cap in hand like Proggy Brien, the beggarman? Yes, Mr Byrne, sir, here's your nation back for you; what way would you like it wrapped?

But other fellows, like Rutch Kelly and his cronies, whose reasons for volunteering had never been clear, were affected by the growing awareness of this *we ourselves*, Sinn Féin, business. They'd become more amenable to drilling correctly, to punctuality and taking orders. Each man had his own gun — though still without ammunition — and carried it well.

As we moved through the spring of '21, the cause, though not yet on the brink of success, made steady progress. Political rule was being wrenched from the Crown, and control of law too, like a beast at a Borris fair, was changing hands. Republican courts at parish, district and higher-up levels listened to complaints and dished out justice. The enemy had lost sway. More and more people bypassed the Crown and came to us to have their complaints dealt with. And our law enforcers were scrupulous in carrying out the court's findings.

Maybe not every judgment was perfect, especially if rival parties were reluctant to have their cases heard before our arbitrators. When two local farmers dragged their dispute through the old system, we could ill afford to let the snub pass. A pure-bred bull had broken into a neighbour's field after a cow. When the cow gave birth, the owner of the bull claimed payment for services rendered, and a row broke out between the neighbours. Had they chosen to put their arguments before our local arbitrator, they'd no doubt have received a more amicable judgment than that meted out in their absence. The morning that the case was due to be heard by the Crown, each farmer opened his front door to find half a calf on his doorstep. From then on, every wrangle in our area went before a Republican court.

But like a child playing wheelie, change

had to be kept on the move, or else it might collapse in a heap.

* * *

Only three of us from the company — myself, Mylie and Tommy Doran — would have any say in the plans for our next attack. We'd need back-up, though, from Cumann na mBan: medical aid should any man get shot, and transport to the nearest infirmary, in town. We'd also need help with escape routes, a supply of food and essentials for a few weeks till the heat was off. Again, our only contacts within the women's organization were Hannah Jordan and Miss Antwerp.

To say I was wary of Miss Jordan's friend was to put it kindly. It was all right dealing with the Englishwoman to organize dances, attend meetings and help with run-of-the-mill activities; indeed, she was more than generous to our cause. But having to depend on her in matters of life and death between the IRA and her fellow citizens made me uneasy. If the truth be known, she probably had a picture of the Light Brigade at Balaclava hanging over her bed, and a copy of the 1916 Proclamation on the reverse side — for Mylie's benefit when he'd call.

Where Hannah Jordan was concerned,

however, you could put your life in her hands, no hesitation. So I went to Miss Jordan, told her about the next ambush and asked her to be ready to assist us on the night, and for a while afterwards. We talked over the essentials: a night's refuge and medical supplies in case of wounds. She was as involved in planning the attack as were Mylie Byrne and Tommy Doran. Then I asked her to do something else: to include Miss Antwerp as little as possible in arrangements, please.

She looked at me questioningly. Why not? says she.

I hadn't expected her to question me.

Ah . . . I'm just a bit worried in case word gets back to brigade HQ, I said. They might put a spanner in the works, and we'd end up not going ahead. But when the operation is over and done with, there's hardly much action the CO can then take, bar reprimand us for not getting permission. And seeing as they've been so toothless themselves, they can ill afford to appear heavy-handed towards a company for doing the job they were set up to do.

Miss Jordan never took her gaze off me while I spoke; her eyes regarded me like a sparrowhawk's. Though she didn't say so, the message broke out across her face: she needed my unconditional trust. The least disparagement, too, of her friend might mean a scintilla of doubt had crept in regarding her own loyalty, and the worthiness of our friendship then would surely be undermined. To show trust was the most important thing, and might even turn out to be the making or breaking of the whole plan. The entire operation looked as if it was turning into a personal thing, and had little to do with a captain's job of being responsible for his men's safety. It was as if safety and trust were two faces of a coin that couldn't be seen together.

Anyway, who was this captain fellow but a helpless *spalpeen*, standing before his lady once more to beg for help, yet at the same time showing reluctance to pander to what the lady might think and feel?

When will your ambush take place? says she sharply.

Of course the boy-in-the-yard gave her details of his plans. Instead of mounting our operation, as before, on the main road out of town, we'd divert the Tans and attack them on the back road, near Colclough's old humped-back bridge, at the point where the road narrows and the hedges and grove give us cover. Again, we'd hit them on their way back to town.

I'd very much appreciate it if you would

arrange for more explosives to be left at the railway station like before, I said. To divert the Tans off the main road, we'll have to blow a crater in it, just after the turn-off onto this back road, and to leave a hole big enough to disrupt traffic for a week or two. At that point in the main road, anyway, the surface is already weak from the waters coming off the hill to one side, and Tommy Doran is so delicate with explosives he can make it look like the whole thing has collapsed after the winter torrents and the recent snow melting. We'll need a full week at least, then, to allow the Tans to get their runs regular on the back road.

In order to place extra hands on standby in case of casualties, Hannah Jordan said she'd also have to know the exact day. But since this wasn't yet decided, I replied that I'd keep in touch and let her know in due course. I didn't mention the dugouts myself and Mylie were making near the location of the attack. Nobody else would know of them either. A fellow had to hold back on something, for you never could tell.

Just over the top of a hill in the middle of Colclough's trees, myself and Mylie spent three days hard shovelling to make the four holes big enough to take twenty men. We formed roofs of three-inch-thick planks, with nine inches of soil layered on top, while the floors, walls and roofs were lined with oilcloth folded at the joints and puttied where clout-head nails tacked the lining to laths plugged into the walls. To protect the oilcloth, we sheeted the walls with light strips of timber and spread clay on the floors. Each access hatch, just big enough for a man to get through, was hinged to one of the planks. At last, with the grass sods replaced, the terrain on top showed little sign of having being touched.

They turned out to be good dry places to store explosives, guns and ammunition; I hoped we might get away without ever having to use them as hideouts. The fact that they were on top of a hill also meant they were unlikely to take in groundwater. Each time myself or Mylie went there, we dragged bushes or branches along and left them scattered nearby. We also incorporated breather holes and built access ladders. Everything was in place.

* * *

Though the weather was dry, there was a touch of a harsh north breeze through the darkening air, a right good bite. Another frosty night lay ahead, unless that breeze picked up. It matched the unease we felt.

Rutch Kelly laid down his gun, sat back on his hunkers and wrapped his arms about himself. Jerry Tobin had also freed his hands to cup and blow into them. We lay in wait for the next twenty minutes, watching for the signal from our look-out up the road. The dread of having forgotten something was like a stone weight inside my head. But it was too late for adjustments: those cursed lorries were due any moment now.

For the thousandth time, I felt for the whistle that hung on a bootlace round my neck. Though I kept my fist tightly closed about it for a while, the thing stayed cold to the touch — the damned chill that evening penetrated everything. The next time I'd finger the shiny metal would be to place it in my mouth to launch the attack. The plunger would go down, and we'd shelter under the dry arch of the bridge for a minute to avoid the falling debris. Then we'd climb the short slope and rise above the stone parapet to fire on any living thing that moved and bore the slightest resemblance to a Black and Tan.

And still we waited. This time all the men, except Tommy Doran, were at the same side of the road — the bank on the other side was too steep for access. Since Tommy Doran was the best shot, I'd positioned him across on a rise of ground where he had a bird's-eye view of proceedings, especially the offside of the lorries, and he could pick off any Tans who went round to outflank us. To help guard our backs, another man with a rifle was placed on the hill to our rear. He'd keep us covered if we had to retreat.

Again I'd called on Mylie Byrne's brother, Will, and sent him way up one end of the road. Since the lorries would come the opposite way, it was just a precaution: a thing or nothing you'd have in your head, something that I hadn't bothered to mention to Mylie, Tommy Doran or Miss Jordan even.

The week before, Tommy Doran had blown up the main road, and the Tans had switched their route as expected. Despite the diversion and shoddier road surface, they'd already managed to establish a pattern: morning and evening runs were almost on schedule.

As the first lorry was about to cross the bridge, we'd blow Horny Han and the crew skyward — the closest to heaven she'd ever get. By then the second lorry, with Angel Annie at the wheel, would be twenty yards behind — the one detail we'd checked carefully each evening. Half the men, under Mylie Byrne's control, were positioned near the second lorry at the moment of the first explosion, and the road was mined there, too.

After that, grenades would become the main weapon, and from then on it would be mostly shotguns and close-quarter stuff.

Standing just under the dry arch, Jerry Tobin again cupped hands round his mouth, but never took his eyes off the plunger. This time it was his job to blow the bridge. The charge had been set only an hour before: we'd sunk holes in the stonework joints of the main arch the previous evening, immediately after the Tan patrol had passed. It was said that Colclough's bridge was hundreds of years old. Ah well, what the hell! Building it back up would provide work for a few men.

At that moment, it dawned on me what was affecting Jerry Tobin and Rutch Kelly. Their hands weren't shivering simply from the cold; they were suffering a touch of that other blasted affliction, the jitters, which kept many a great man down. At its worst, the problem was known to freeze soldiers to the spot, and prevent them going over the top after whistle-blow. It had better not hold our men back! While my own hands were steady enough, something was weighing on my brain. I could even feel the damned thing pressing on my insides, like rocks in the gut.

What in heaven's name was I doing there anyway, fighting for freedom yet about to destroy what every man had a right to: the freedom to breathe? And not just the lives of those Tan bastards — that was bad enough — but it could also spell the end for the men I'd led into this. One detail overlooked, of either training or equipment, might mean the death of those who'd trusted me not to make such an error. Grave as it was, the prospect had to be faced: some of our lads — even that coon Rutch Kelly — mightn't survive the attack. I looked at Jerry Tobin's hands and willed them to stop shaking. His eyes, thankfully, stayed fixed on the plunger. I looked up the road towards Mylie Byrne. He spotted me and appeared to grin back — he had the finest set of crockery of any man I knew.

I hoped he'd get to tickle Miss Antwerp with that big moustache again. And which way, this evening, was her picture facing — the one that, I was sure, hung on the wall of her bedroom? I also wished I hadn't said anything to Hannah Jordan about her. *All in the valley of Death / Rode the six hundred* — could Rutch Kelly recite that poem? Or maybe sing it to the air of *She is far from the land*, in his big tenor voice.

If I could only take myself and the men away from this valley, out of this fix. But it was too late for that: everything from here on was in the hands of fate. Against the sound of rushing water, it was hard to keep from nodding off.

The place spurted to life. Sharp whistling came from one end of the road, and young Will Byrne waved like mad. Why was he signalling? The Tans would come from the opposite end, any second now — get back to your post, you little twerp! But the look-out up the other end had started to wave as well.

This wasn't meant to be. Tans approaching from both directions? I'd barely got the whistle to my mouth, when the rumble of lorries rose above the sound of the Urrin river rushing under the main arch of the bridge. It was annoying to find my body reacting so slowly to an instruction from my head. The sleep-inducing sound of the water must've overcome my ears and the whiff of a turf fire down the valley seeped up my nose and captured whatever bit of brain was in there.

The men were as bad: they were reacting so slowly. I whistled again. Mylie stood on the hedgerow up the road like he was about to go for a stroll of a summer's day. I tried to signal Tommy Doran over on the far rise of ground. What had got into everybody to make them so slow? Then Jerry Tobin climbed across the parapet of the bridge. For feck's sake!

Get back here, I shouted at him. Why are you going onto the road?

To get the explosive, says he.

He'd barely climbed over the parapet when his body gave a jerk and the crack of a rifle came from somewhere. I looked up. I didn't see Tans, only lorries approaching from either direction. But Tommy Doran's rifle, it seemed, was pointing towards us. It couldn't be, *surely*.

At last, my body began to do what it was bid and to move quickly. Mylie was drawing his section back. I hopped up onto the bridge, picked up Jerry Tobin — he was a small enough man — and dropped him over to Rutch Kelly.

For a second in the middle of the tumult, I caught Kelly's eye on me: utter contempt showed in his face. I'd never seen it so clearly expressed before, a full-frontal look of hatred, something he'd never let go of. The bastard had taken this chance, when I was liable to get hit, to show how he felt. *Good riddance!* was written all over his face. What I'd hoped had faded to a scintilla, or died away altogether over the last two years, was back as strong as ever, eating him up. I can't explain it, but I got a weird, almost brutish, satisfaction at seeing him like this; that my expectation of him had been fulfilled — once a beast always a beast.

I stood there for a moment defying him,

inviting him to come out from safety and stand on the bridge in the open to see who'd take the first bullet. Had he the guts to match his hatred? At last, I'd shaken off the uncertainties that had earlier clutched at my insides. It was gratifying, almost exhilarating, to see clearly who my enemies were.

Climbing over the parapet again, I felt a *zip* past my head, and heard a *zing* off the top of the wall nearby, then another rifle crack.

There was plenty of time to move through the wood and up to the dugouts, I reckoned. The lorries were approaching the bridge only very slowly. In low gear, three engines ground their way down each hill, growling like an empty corn-mill. Intent on reaching the bridge, a handful of regular troops — your plain tommies were let face the risks — crouched and moved closely beside each lorry. I didn't see as much as one Tan out front; they huddled along behind the lorries.

We got all the men into the dugouts, and lowered Jerry Tobin. To make sure no telltale signs were left behind, myself and Mylie stayed above; then we crept back to the top of the brow and, through the trees, watched the enemy capers below at the bridge for a minute or two.

At that moment, I remembered Tommy Doran. There was no sign of him. With so many troops, he probably hadn't been able to cross the road. I'd told him about the dugouts, but he didn't know exactly where they were. Anyway, he ought to have had enough savvy to lie low for a few days and not return home: the peelers would surely have his name. It looked like we'd all become marked men, with no choice but to go on the run full-time.

But something else about Tommy Doran bothered me. I had this picture of him pointing a gun in our direction just after Jerry Tobin was shot, though I hadn't seen one enemy by that stage. Not only that, he'd failed to make it back. Could I dare suspect him?

Come on, says Mylie, nudging me. It's time we made ourselves scarce: some of them might've gone round the back of us.

At least Mylie had kept his cool. To be taken from behind is the most unnerving prospect for any soldier. Before rising to my knees, I turned to scan the ditches around to check for movement. Just before we left, the rat-tat of a Vickers sent a barrage of bullets into tree boles, spattering and sprinkling the carpet of deadwood on the ground, there since the previous year's growth. Suddenly the thicket just below us was hit. Time indeed to make ourselves scarce.

All that pleasure of thinking I'd identified my enemies, while defying Rutch Kelly below on the bridge, was about as cold then as a yesterday's dinner. Thoughts of the unseen enemy among us sent shivers through me again as we lowered the hatch and went to earth.

12

We must have traipsed five miles along the riverbed in the dark. Jerry Tobin was weak from loss of blood, and I was tired from carrying him. He groaned, half in and half out of consciousness. Although I wasn't sure, I didn't reckon his wound was fatal; it was in the lower left side of the gut, and the bullet had gone clean through. But such an amount of blood as he'd lost, despite our efforts to stem the gush, must have weakened him seriously, and there was also the dread of infection.

Why the hell hadn't he left the explosive where it was? I hoped the determination and grit of the little man when he'd got such a fixation would now stand him in good stead. One or two of the others wanted to help carry him, but it was better this way. Tobin trusted me to look after him, and faith was a precious thing, as fragile as gossamer of late September — especially when it came to deciding whether to carry on or not.

We couldn't afford to stop to rest. The wounded man needed medical attention urgently. And we had to reach Killoughrim

Wood, where we could lie up for days, for weeks. Given that Miss Antwerp's house was close by, we might manage to get essentials and, through her, stay in touch with the world outside. I'd no choice but to depend on her now; though since Jerry Tobin had been shot — the moment before I'd looked up to see Tommy Doran pointing his gun our way — it seemed she may not've been the traitor after all. But first we'd have to get there without being followed. Since the Tans were known to use bloodhounds, and they'd surely have a pack on our tails down on the train from Dublin by morning, we trudged along the middle of the river-bed and avoided the banks at all times.

Earlier, with the covers closed, the only light we'd had in the dugouts was from candles. We'd left the spaces too small, with the result that the cluster of heads looked more like spectres packed into graves than soldiers on the run. It gave me reason to wonder if the dugouts had been such a good idea: maybe we should've made a run for it rather than be cooped up in holes, like rabbits waiting stock-still for hunters to dig them out. The fear had shown on our candlelit faces and filled the silent tomb. Then, none too soon, came the moment to chance pushing back the cover, when we looked up into a glorious midnight-blue sky dotted with flickering light flecks, and filled with the novelty of first sighting, an almost magical experience, I emerged — crept out — into that wonderful universe. There was neither sight nor sound of Tan or tommy, or their lorries. Freedom in the blue night had the taste and smell of a world apart, and within a few minutes I was back to give the men the all-clear.

So relieved to be on the go again, I hardly minded the river betimes up to my waist. And it was just as well this wasn't a week earlier, or the river would've been impassable: full from the snow melting on the hills. The mad March moon gave us just enough light to pick out one another's bulk against the soft gleam of water, and the cold and endless slurp-slurping was a small price to pay for the delight of the night's freedom. With Colclough's bridge well behind us, Killoughrim Wood was getting nearer.

The river was well into the forest before we left it. Having clambered up through briars and willows on the bank, at last we could collapse safely on the floor of the wood. Nature's womb had opened up to take its children back to itself, solacing as well as giving refuge. Neither time nor Tans had influence in here, where such things as frenzy and turmoil were alien. No doubt I'd have stayed for goodness knows how long, but for pressing business.

Myself and Mylie carried Jerry Tobin on the paths we remembered from days gone by, till we arrived at a clearing by a field near Miss Antwerp's house. Before returning to lead the others to the house, Mylie went ahead to give notice that we had a man for urgent dressing and nourishment. Once we'd dried ourselves, we could at least rest in comfort for the remainder of the night — in the loft where we'd stayed on the night of the hooley.

As with the dugouts, I hadn't told Tommy Doran of this escape route either. And was I glad? I tried to put him out of my head; the trouble that each hour brought was enough for the time being. And whenever anger got to me, I kept the lid on by repeating to myself: ex, or non-ex, British soldier, you, Mr Tommy Doran, will be dealt with later.

Miss Antwerp and two other women had waited up for us. Even though I'd asked her not to, Hannah Jordan must've relayed our plans. So who else knew? Without the least sign of tiredness, they buzzed round us and took charge of Jerry Tobin, laid him gently on the long kitchen table and propped him with pillows. Having cleaned his wound and bandaged it as best they could, they picked dry clothes from a tea chest full of cast-offs and deftly dressed him, then spooned soup and hot chocolate into him. I could've robbed him of it.

The rest of our company, bar one, had arrived, and crouched as near as they could get to the great open fire in the kitchen. A mighty pot-black cooking stove nearby was also roaring, and tiny pools of water sizzled on its plates as drips fell from the coats, shirts, waistcoats and pairs of trousers that hung on the airing-racks overhead. Decorum had gone by the wayside: there was not a man among us who wasn't cold, bedraggled and tired. And Mylie Byrne looked the worst of all; his face gone grey, he shivered inside the blanket Miss Antwerp had placed over his shoulders. But more than anything else that rasping cough of his sounded none too healthy. How could men be expected to spend more than one night in the open? We hadn't trained for what the situation had thrown up.

And all for nothing. Not so much as one blooming shot had been fired at the enemy. Heaven save any nation from depending on a mob of amateurs to attain its freedom. And what hope would there have been if we'd had to go hand-to-hand with the enemy? A fair number of these decent men would surely have fallen. Was any cause worth this?

I hadn't the heart to ask one among them to accompany Jerry Tobin to the infirmary in town. Two women wrapped him in tartan rugs, loaded him up and set off down the carriageway. Miss Antwerp drove the pony and trap — complete with hissing carbide lamps — while one of her friends cradled the invalid. I rode her father's bike alongside, holding on to the headboard till we got out on to the open road, and then rode ahead to make sure the way was clear. The two revolvers, one in each pocket, were still sticking out through the lining of my short coat.

We had your man safely ensconced in the infirmary within the hour. Nurses who knew nurses who were in the women's movement flapped us away, and then wheeled him off down a long corridor. At last, Jerry Tobin's welfare was in the best of hands.

On our way in, I'd noticed a shed and outhouses to the rear of the infirmary. So rather than head back with Miss Antwerp, I handed her the pair of revolvers to give to Mylie Byrne, and took myself round there to find a dry spot to lay my head on for a while.

* * *

While I knew you were a nurse, Lucy Brien, it didn't occur to me that you might've been working there in the infirmary, and you might even have been on duty that night; for I would surely have made it my business to bump into you. Would you have been pleased to see me? We scarcely knew each other then, of course, but how could I ever forget you from the night we'd met in the loft?

It must please you, though, to know that our daughter is following in your footsteps as a nurse; not in the infirmary (you'll be glad about that): she works in the mental hospital on the other side of town. That's also where Rutch Kelly's son, the doctor, works — the lad didn't get that talent from his father.

Two fine boys you produced before you upped and left us. Jem looks a lot like you now. If ever there was a bond between mother and son, or mother and first-born, it was between you two; without saying a word, you seemed to know what was in each other's head.

Your passing affected him more than the rest of us. The loss in his life has since been filled — with work: Sunday and Monday, from early morning till after dark. He's the sheep farmer now. Apart from our own few acres here round the house and our grazing rights on the mountain commons, Jem leases a good deal of land from farmers below on the flatlands. I've taken to drawing the old-age pension — and not the old-IRA pension either, mind. I do the cooking and potter with the yard work; then to town on the bus of a Friday to get the meat from Liam Dempsey for a good Sunday stew. Once or twice a week, depending on the weather, I like to take a walk across the mountain for a few hours to stretch my legs.

Our other fellow, Martin (though we named him after your father, he reminds me of my own father), has long since flown the nest. Married and living in town, he too has followed your footsteps into nursing. When established, he helped our Sarah to get a placement as a trainee in the asylum. All three of them are set up for life, and don't tell me you had no hand or part in any of this.

But is it not a little bit peculiar all the same that, since the night I brought Jerry Tobin to the infirmary, I've had my fair share of links with hospitals? And at least one of those links was that strange, wonderful and never-to-be forgotten experience: the time I spent recuperating in a storeroom and you were my . . . nurse — you know very well what I'm on about, Lucy Brien.

13

It was well on in the day when I woke, got up and shook off the straws. Being in the vicinity, I thought I'd take a wander through the town and down to the barracks, to see if there was any stir from the RIC after the previous night. The Tan lorries had been left parked near the barracks — and so what were the local boys doing these days that they couldn't place a stick of explosive under a lorry, light a short fuse and run? By heaven, there was a time in this town when the enemy wouldn't be let do what he liked.

The shops were open and the streets were stirring. I dallied to absorb the smell of business, that flurry of shuffle, mid-morning packaging and unpacking by men in aprons. It was a chance to forget myself as I gawped at the items on display, while taking in from the corner of my eye the capers of clerks behind counters, especially where a window opened to afford a good look. But more mesmerizing still were the shapes of bodkin-haired browsers in floor-sweeping skirts and nice tight bodices, who casually inspected the wares of the day, as if the same goods were totally new or hadn't been seen a day or two previous, the last time they'd called. I tried to figure out if the ladies were aware that the ogling eyes of a country *cábóg* outside were fixed on them, and if not how much movement on my part did it take to distract their attention. More than just amusement, it was a way of tying myself into the town's morning life to make sure that I really wasn't still in the middle of last night, merely dreaming.

A few yards up the street, a sweeper took a shovel and brush together from his handcart and banged them on the kerb in temper. A horse had shifted its weight off one leg, cocked its tail and fouled the roadway, and was being ignored by the driver, who chatted to a shopkeeper taking a break from behind his counter. Over in the open space near the centre of the Square, a mason's apprentice flung bricks in pairs from a large stack into his wooden barrow — so far the only specimen in the area who looked like he was interested in work. But my opinion would soon change: at the opposite side of the Square I came across a two-horse dray, and three men sweated and parbuckled mighty butts and hogsheads down a pair of wooden ramps onto the pavement, then down to a cellar underneath.

I walked the pavements riveted by what I'd always thought was the best part of life there, the only reason, indeed, why streets should be. It was a pity that once the day ended, all workers couldn't go out and reside in the countryside decently, like so many of their employers, leaving the town locked up good and proper behind them, instead of having to undergo the night cooped up in parcels. I felt a shiver at the thought of such a life; unable to see the horizon and with all that smoke hanging about in heavy weather and winter, a body would never waken to the bawl of cattle, or hear the *stumph* of bumblebees on knapweed in high summer.

By hanging about and becoming lost amid the novelty of shop and street business I was trying to distance myself for a while from the previous night, but thoughts of the goings-on lurked at the edges, like dark clouds, threatening to swamp my brain. So it was best that I immediately got on with the business at hand, my purpose for staying overnight in the vicinity. But before going near the barracks, I decided I'd walk up past the church to the top of the town, just to clear my lungs.

Then I stopped a familiar face in the distance. Your man's brother, Bobby Doran, was coming down the far side of the street. Feeling suddenly tense, I turned away to follow him in the nearest shop window. He stopped, pulled out what appeared to be a mauve envelope from his inside coat-pocket and smoothed it against his leg. He passed down and entered, of all places, the premises of a well-known unionist — loyalist, royalist or monarchist, call him what you will — the same merchant whom Rutch Kelly had once relieved of his antique weapons. An old foe planted in a prime location on our street, the unionist was one of Cromwell's seed and a member of that hard-nosed hard-hat brigade who, only because they defied all links with where they lived other than to make money, were looked on as foe. They saw themselves as English — even after hundreds of years — although they were really no more than a pathetic shower of snooty-nosed *boolimskees*. And this boy was one such skulker, suspected of passing information to Crown forces. But what business did Bobby Doran have going in there?

The merchant didn't entertain him for long — you can bet he didn't. Out they both came, stood on the sloped doorstep and had a few words before Doran went back up the way he'd come. The other man watched him; then he took something from his pocket — ah, it was that mauve envelope — and went inside. Would I ever be so lucky as to have stumbled across something? I'd wait till Doran had taken himself far up the street and out of sight: I didn't want to meet him.

The next minute, the merchant reappeared on the doorstep. With that dire thing, the bowler hat on, he tugged at the lapels of his velvet-collared greatcoat. Then, chisel-faced to match, he marched down the pavement with the crisp walk of the wide-boy businessman that he most certainly was — and with no pretensions of Puritan practice either. Past the Corner House Hotel, along the bottom of the Square, past the Athenaeum and down by the Castle, he went. I took my time following him, just in case. As expected, he turned in at the door of the RIC barracks. It was only then that I ran to catch up.

Without thinking about it, I turned in at the same door. I had to find evidence that what I'd begun to suspect was being borne out: that the two Doran brothers were passing information to the police by way of a middleman. So severe would be the consequences for the brothers that I just had to make sure their hands were dirty. Being of a different ilk, the merchant would be dealt with in another way — execution was too honourable a fate for his likes. But he would not last in business beyond the end of the year.

As things turned out I was barely in time. A bearded constable was in the act of removing the mauve envelope from the counter as I pushed open the swing door and brazened it right up to him. The merchant turned on his heels and walked out, the constable brought the letter to an inner office and I was left standing. In a few minutes, a half-dozen police came tearing out from a corridor, pulling on tunic coats and fixing regulation caps, and swept past me like I was furniture. The bastards had rifles too.

The fellow on desk-duty returned, checked his day-book, picked up and nibbed a slender pen, dipped it in ink and wrote for surely five minutes. I might as well have been a shadow across the floor: not once did he so much as look in my direction, and I was tempted to walk away. At the same time, this status gave me subtle liberties. I could lift my head, look all round and take things in — you never knew, the information might come in handy some time. The corridor almost behind the desk counter, the inside of the front door and south-facing windows were heavily barred; the place was a fortress. Still, I thought, Tommy Doran would bung a hole through with his explosives — Damn it, I'd forgotten:

he wouldn't do any such thing.

Well, what's your business here? a voice asked.

For two reasons I didn't answer him right away. First of all, I wasn't sure it was your man before me who'd spoken: he hadn't lifted his head, so I hadn't seen his lips move. Secondly, the voice was so casual it seemed unlikely he was talking to me; I had to work it out. But there was nobody else present. He could hardly be hiding anyone below the desk, and he wasn't speaking into a telephone piece.

Are you deaf as well as dishevelled? came the voice again.

I lowered my head to grovel as best I could, but focused my eyes only below desk level — to watch him. Was he carrying a piece, and how many others were down the corridor? I didn't know what he meant by *dishevelled*; no doubt it had something to do with my unkempt look, though his own face could've done with a shave. His beard was spiked out like the head of a bottlebrush. If I looked untidy, I might be taken for a travelling labourer. Yeah, that was it: I'd pass myself off nicely as a *spalpeen* drifting through, looking for work with the first respectable farmer who'd pay an honest wage. And since half the country was in turmoil, what better place for a travelling man to enquire about the work round about than at the local barracks?

Oh, I'm sorry to bother you, sir, says I — the peelers loved it when people grovelled. I'll not trouble you no further. I'm in search of a kind farmer with a bit of spring work to offer. There's awful unrest, sir, over in Cork and Tipperary and no work no more. Some places are worse than others, with wild men on the loose, shooting and killing decent people. I was wondering if there's any trouble in these parts, sir. I'd like to give all them places a wide berth. Tell me, sir, are there any places round about here like that?

The bottlebrush in tunic raised its ugly head to study me. We had some slight disturbance last night, says he. Out towards the mountains, but it's nothing serious. We're on our way there now to catch us a few Shinners in their hidey-hole.

Oh, that's grand so, says I. Not much trouble in these parts. I turned to leave, and on my way out I called back to him: Oh, I hope you catch them fellows.

Don't worry, he shouted back. We'll get our hands on them.

Like hell you will, says I to myself. I'd meet the man in town some time and put him in his hidey-hole for good.

The Tan lorries had arrived as I went out,

and engines chugged in wait for Horny Han and Angel Annie to press pedals and steer them off in column formation towards the mountains. Walking from their billets in good loyalist households, no doubt, round the town, Tans and Auxies alike were late; they almost looked human as they brushed their hair before fixing peaked caps and floppy tams on their heads. They'd probably gone on a late binge — maybe they'd needed to — after the disruption of the previous evening's routine: *Chasing a gang of damned Shinners off a bridge out near the mountains, we was: troublesome lot*. Pity whichever poor innkeeper had to tolerate such poultices the previous night, and dole out free drink, while looking down the barrel of a Long Webley. If the war were to go on, every decent publican in this town would go bust from handing out drink to that lowlife.

I didn't have much time. I strolled past them, hoping they wouldn't pick on me: those sons of bastards could start their little games. As soon as they were out of view, I began to run.

Up past the Castle and into the Square, I went. The first car I came across with the motor running was a Model T Ford, with a tall middle-aged man sitting behind the wheel. The last time I'd been that close to a

Model T was when myself and Tommy Doran removed the trembler coils from the local doctor's car; we'd had need of them, in addition to a few flash-lamp batteries, to make devices for setting off explosives. We were sorry it'd had to be the doc's car, but he kept a horse, which he used for his rounds and which was more dependable anyway than these newfangled machines, he'd always said.

By this time, I'd taken off my coat so as not to appear *dishevelled* — as Constable Bottlebrush had put it — and I stayed in near the car so the driver wouldn't see the state of my trousers and boots. By my coming on him suddenly, he wouldn't have time to weigh up the brazen commoner; surprise, like the motorcar, is a great device, and I'll be damned if the trick didn't work.

Is she as good as a pony? says I, striking up a conversation.

She's cheaper than a steed, says he. Quite reliable, too, once you get to know her eccentricities. And indeed, I might add, not nearly as moody as a female. Haw, haw.

Another hoity-toity comic. In tweeds, cap and cravat, he was as posh as a bank manager, and proud as a peacock on a zinc roof displaying its finery to hens. He just sat there lording it. A grand pair of stitched leather gloves rested themselves on the other front seat. Oh, but I could've done with such items the previous night.

In that case, you won't mind taking me for a spin, says I.

Times of emergency bring out a fiendish pleasure in humankind, and I'd changed from the head-bowed friendly boot-licker of a few minutes earlier to a drastic zealot on a mission — and liked the change, the flamboyance. I hopped in beside your man, poked him in the ribs with a finger through my coat pocket, letting on it was a revolver, and told him to get a move on.

Mr Peacock went stiff and, without his gloves, put his hands on the wheel, gave the pedal a dig of his right boot, and we shot off up the street.

Can you not go any faster? says I, when we were about two miles out of town. Get out quick, or I'll shoot you.

Tweeds and all, the poor man was left dumbstruck on the side of the road as I took over at the wheel. Driving away, I turned my head to savour the look of him one more time. I don't know which he was most afraid of: me or the thought of having his precious black beauty turned into a wreck. His fists pushed upwards against the chin as if he were trying to force his mouth shut, even though there wasn't so much as a cheep out of him.

By the time he'd have pulled himself together, gone back to the barracks and reported me, I'd have reached Miss Antwerp's to warn the boys.

I hadn't had much experience behind the wheel, except for the few times with Mylie Byrne on the mill lorry out delivering timber, when we'd changed places and he'd shown me how to drive. The gears were near enough the same, but balancing the foot pedals was the problem. The Model T spluttered and jerked forward, but luckily it didn't cut out. With gears tearing, I drove the hell off with myself. A lot lighter to steer than the mill lorry, the car hopped along like a herring on a griddle — I'd have to concentrate hard to hold this beauty between the ditches. It reminded me of a film I'd seen in the picture-house once when, at the end, a fellow disappears over the hill, his open-top hopping along the centre of the road.

Up the Republic, I roared back at your man, as the road fell away behind.

14

I went hooting up the driveway like I was landed gentry letting the servants know it was time to dance attendance. And by the time I got the motor to slow down near the front entrance, wheels ploughing ruts through the pebbles, Miss Antwerp and Mylie were on the doorstep to see the commotion.

With his thumb, Mylie flicked up his hat to scratch his forehead — the same habit as when he'd worn a cap; the hat was a recent fad, since he'd met Miss Antwerp. He must've borrowed it from her father: he'd been wearing a cap the night before. 'Twas nice to see the colour back in his face.

There was certainly a sense of occasion, and surprise, to my arriving there in such style. The lord and lady of the manor were out to greet their cousin dropping by in his new motorcar.

Miss Antwerp must've read my mind, given that she laughed: And will our guest do us the honour of gracing our table for tea? Indeed, might we persuade you to stay overnight?

What ho, perhaps so — I tried the accent. Overnight? Are we having a party: a spot of piano, fiddle and tenor? How about a game or two of bridge in the morning room to pass a late hour, and ride out after breakfast?

And a touch of croquet on the lawn in the afternoon? says she.

Awfully sorry, my dear, I would love to oblige, but I must push on. I've got some pressing business with His Lordship, if he will spare me a word.

Not letting go of the game already begun, she brushed aside my apologies and pressing business. The woman wasn't so easily dismissed.

Squire Byrne licked his lips and looked at Miss Antwerp with the eyes of a pet lamb seeking its bottle at feeding time. *I'd* love a touch of croquet, says he. Sporting a great grin on his face, he stood with his arm round the lady's shoulder, as if he'd never known any other way to live, hadn't looked like a drowned rat or coughed like he'd been on his last legs with consumption a few short hours before.

Would you indeed, Myles? says Miss Antwerp, with a slight tang.

Aye, Myles, I know the croquet you have in mind, says I.

Oh, that, says she, is old hat. We've been bashing our mallet and ball about already this morning, haven't we, Myles?

But Mylie had a way of handling the sting in her tail. Is that what you'd call it? says he.

The picture, with sound added, was an eyeful to relish: frozen in time like a sepia snap from a shoebox under the bed. Despite the lorries of damnation closing in, every sign of urgency was shelved for this all-too-brief lull. So lazily did we skit each other, you'd imagine there was all the time in the world. And so alluring was it that I found myself opening the car door to swing my legs out with the ease of a dandy fop.

The skitting intensified to become outlandish, a lovely wicked thing. And the rapport strengthened; grew special, almost ideal — well, I, at least, had seldom tasted its like. Though the merriment pushed close to mocking bawdiness, not once did we cross the line, defy good form and propriety or become crude. Such was the three-way regard. It was as if we knew precisely one another's worth to the moment — and, bejabers, does that ever give satisfaction!

The instant was mighty: we three were in it, carrying a certain nervous electric charge with us. That's not to say that the fate looming wasn't of itself reason enough for nervous strain, but the charge was rooted in the bowels: it was primitive, and the tension it produced had to do with something altogether different from the threat of Tans.

Myself and Mylie knew we would never have dared enter the grounds of such a place as this other than to poach the odd salmon from the river or cull a little game — in or out of season — never mind stand before its manor house, act grand and take liberties with notions of old decency. Yet here we were doing just this, making the place our own and enjoying it without qualm. What's more, this station wasn't one bit beyond us: a little tutoring from Her Ladyship and we could lord it with the highest nobs in the land, genteel or otherwise — and, sure, by the gait of Mylie he was already halfway on the road to gentility.

Were we indeed to take over the whole estate and manor, how different would our actions be from that of any planter gone before us, for whom might was ever right. But we had more claim to this piece of rich earth. Our ancestors had been here first, before the trees were cut. Wouldn't we only be colonizing our own soil?

Things coming about full circle, opposites being joined or whatever else causes electric charges, could've very well accounted for the excitement in myself and Squire Byrne. But Miss Antwerp was a different kettle of fish. So at a moment of danger, what made her spark?

I had to admit that Miss Antwerp was proving to be a person totally different from how I had seen her before. Not only was she a settler — and an English one at that, who occupied the spot where a native's wattle-and-daub, and later a mud-wall cabin, had once stood in the forest clearing — she was fornicating with one of our fighting men. And, to complicate matters, she'd come over to our side and taken such an active part in our war as must surely have put her under the eye of the peelers. Indeed, through this action alone, she may well have surpassed myself and Mylie in our rebel activities. Such disparity as she carried with her was maybe what gave the moment its greatest charge. And, what's more, it didn't half take guts for a woman to drop the hoity-toity and disdain of her class, change sides and throw her lot in with some ragged underdog, republican foe.

She certainly didn't deceive by means of her appearance. With hardly the shapeliest of ankles and being a touch plump beyond sylphlike, she was unlikely to become a soldier's dream of ideal womanhood, his usual female figurehead of unmated queen. The other lady, Hannah Jordan, for her looks alone would've made a better model.

It was all very well to imagine a new nation in the guise of some winsome colleen, but more earthy ingredients were called for in this war. So Miss Antwerp's presence began to have new meaning for me. At a time when trust outranked religion, looks or the king's shilling, it could at least be said of Miss Antwerp: The woman can be trusted. And no better tribute might be paid to a living soul on either this island or the other. I couldn't think of anybody I knew who demonstrated better than Miss Antwerp the defiance and courage vital to harbour in the pits of a republic's new gut — despite where she'd come from. How could I ever have doubted her?

But like the moments before midnight, time was fast running out. For what had begun as a hum in the distance had become a definite drone, and was changing to the growl of engines coming near: much louder than the sparking plugs and rattle of the black beauty chugging away beneath me.

Tan lorries, I shouted. Quick! Get the lads out to the wood, I roared at Mylie. The peelers know where we are. They'll appear up that drive any minute.

I had barely slowed for an instant of fun, it seemed, before I had to swing black beauty about through the pebbles and head down the drive. Without stopping, I turned her onto the road and sped off in the opposite direction to town. After about a mile, I took a left fork and then a lane branching off that.

I dumped the car over the brow of a field. 'Twould be a while before Mr Tweeds would place his gloves on the front seat again.

15

The world was a different place by the time I got back to the Antwerps'. The Tans had arrived, parked their lorries in front of the house and set about their business. The horror had begun. Fire.

Smoke rose from the yard at the back. Shed and outhouses, as well as the barn and loft we'd danced in, were being eaten up in flames: scarlet, orange and lemon tongues darted upwards, as if chasing their lesser brother, smoke. I was mesmerized; numbed more than horrified at the sight.

I had to shake my body from its stupor and do something — but what? I hopped over the wall and moved behind the tree trunks, edging as close as I could get to the house. Having to skulk felt like hairs growing under my tongue, and such action meant I was about as useful as a frail old dodderer.

I moved from behind the last tree, ran across the open driveway — dared that much, at least — and swung across the low metal railing Mylie had hopped over the evening we'd sauntered up there. Then I made it to the grove on the far side, which ran nearer the house.

Most of the Tans had been round the back, but had started returning to the front of the house. The vile creatures were everywhere. Two groups of three came marching down the drive and passed close to me, on their way to the front gate — easy targets, if only I'd had a revolver. In their part-soldiers' and part-policemen's uniforms — dark-green tunics, black belts and khaki trousers — they marched stiffly up and down the road like Christmas toys.

At least our men had got away in time.

Now that they had burned down what they must've thought was the rebels' retreat — we Shinners were who the Tans were after — they surely wouldn't do anything more to the Antwerps?

Miss Antwerp and her father were being held roughly, as if they were beasts or native Irish, and questioned by two officers — if you could call them such. One fellow raised his arm and gave Miss Antwerp a slap across the face with his open hand. But it had the opposite effect on her demeanour: she stuck her head in the air and spat into his eyes. The fellow laughed — more a sneer than a laugh — turned away from her, but then suddenly swung round again and, with all his might, punched her in the stomach. She bent over for a short time only before straightening herself up again, despite the pain. The woman had the courage of two men — certainly more than those two low thugs. If the Doran brothers could see what they'd brought down on this fair maiden's head, and feel the chill of their handiwork, would they be so fond of passing information? The numbness and shock I'd felt was being replaced by a growing anger, or fear — it was hard to tell the difference.

Next thing, there was a sound of breaking glass: something had been thrown through the ground-floor window on the left, into what I believe they called the drawing room. We'd heard the piano from under a partially raised bottom sash of that same window one evening only a couple of years before. Miss Antwerp had then heaved the sash higher, leaned out on the sill, and given Mylie a grin secret from the rest of us. In fun, we'd gone down on our knees, stretched out our arms and thumped our chests to mock the concert inside. At the memory of that event, its sudden brilliance, I felt a shiver across my shoulders.

Strangely, the breaking glass was not unlike some of the piano notes we heard that evening, as if glass and piano sounds were thwarting each other across time. In my head I could hear Kelly's tenor voice again.

Smoke came from the window. It drifted at first, gradually increased, and then rose up in the air in search of its evil cousin already over the yard, the black demon of an early-afternoon sky. There came another sound of glass breaking: one more ground-floor window gone in. Yet more smoke.

Once the fire took hold in that tinderbox, it was only minutes before it gnawed its way upwards. The Tans had showed what they were made of, proved what the reports had said and what we'd come to expect of them. We'd hoped against hope that none of it had been true — but it was. I couldn't believe, though, that they'd set fire to a house of one of their fellow citizens.

Miss Antwerp's face was no longer visible. Tangled hair fell and covered her features. I couldn't tell if she was crying — I didn't want her to. Being held there, she looked as wild and primitive as I imagined any maternal ancestor of mine before being taken behind the wattle-and-daub to be pinned down and violated. Nothing new, it was ever this way: violence and bleeding being at the heart of recreation.

'Cept this time, I felt such a foul dismay I might have been on the attacking side myself, one of the pillagers after the spoils. By involving Miss Antwerp in the company's activities, exposing her to traitors and finally abandoning her to these thugs, I had condemned her and the old man to their brutal fates. The fear I'd had before was turning to guilt and nausea in my gut, followed by a sharp horror: a sudden foreboding of what next would be visited on the Antwerps. As if a great fist had reached inside and dragged me to the ground, I went down on my knees, and the memories became yet more brilliant, shimmering.

The first time I'd seen this house it seemed to be a cross between a manor and a townhouse. Facing south but angled sideways, it had the air of a great mansion. Your eye would delight in its good looks, low rooflines and classic proportions. Here I was again trying to hold my thumb before my eye to measure the overall height against the overall width; a gesture without thought, it was no more than the attempt a small child might make to wipe away a vision of horror and reinstate some happy picture. One measurement an exact multiple of the other, and the correct width matched its length.

But the horror wouldn't budge. The proud old tinder-box was fast becoming a burning pyre.

The next minute, father and daughter, along with two people who worked there, were set upon by groups of Tans: each victim, apart from the old man, who kept both palms on his stick to prop himself, was pinned from behind, hands pushed upwards on their backs. Then, like pigs being readied for sticking, they were pulled and dragged towards the open door — the same door Hannah Jordan had opened on the night of the party. I could almost hear its clunk again, and the weatherboard drag across the floor.

The entrance to a night's delights had become the archway to a burning cavern.

Miss Antwerp's bearded father, an old codger in an armchair the last time I'd seen him, raised his stick to swipe at one of the thugs. The Tan used his rifle to ward off the blow, and then jabbed the old man under the arm with the bayonet. The old man dropped to his knees. Another thug lifted him and dragged him closer to the door.

When his daughter broke away from her assailants and went to help her father, she too got the prod of a bayonet and went down. She was nabbed from behind once more, and hoisted towards the entrance. All were forced inside. The door was then locked. The fire burned.

I pinched the skin on the backs of my

hands to see their faces and feel their pain — but there was none. The hallway was what came to mind. Quiet and mighty, it had been big enough to fit a small house into. I pictured the great stairs in the centre and the growth of a large brown stain in one corner under the stair landing.

They'll have a job getting rid of that mushroom, Mylie's voice came into my head.

It'll be got rid now, I said.

At last I could envisage them, their bodies — though not their faces. Father and daughter were on their knees just inside the door, their heads pushed as close as possible to the bottom of the weatherboard as they gasped for air. Everything they touched was hot. Stifled and parched, Miss Antwerp licked the tiles running diagonally across the floor, but even they were warm. And instead of that mixture of saline cold and clammy dust she'd hoped for, bits of hot charcoal stuck to her tongue.

If she had thoughts and feelings about anything other than the immediate peril which would end their lives, the destruction of their home must have caused her the most anguish. Would she try to banish these thoughts and instead maybe recall that bubble of bliss when she and Mylie, the lord and lady of the manor, had opened the door there and come out to see who was arriving in the motorcar; when all three of us had seemed so defiantly indestructible? Her memory of those halcyon moments and of Mylie's fondness for her as he tilted her father's hat back on his head, I hoped, would bring her comfort, as would the knowledge that Mylie had got away to the woods in time.

In my mind's eye I saw them in their final terror. It came at them from the crackling of wood all round, but especially from overhead. But when they raised their eyes from the weatherboard to check, all they could see was smoke, getting denser and blacker. Instead of bending down again for air, they panicked and gulped in clouds of poison; coughing till their heads went dizzy, they clasped hands, and the last sense to fail each of them was that of smell before the black treacle-like clouds clogged their noses and they sank into unconsciousness.

With all energy spent, the old man's body was first to fall over. Miss Antwerp subsided but a few seconds after her father. In an instant and before flesh could char on the black and white tiles, their lungs collapsed. The end, I knew, would come by way of suffocation rather than burning.

Still on my knees in the grove, I had heard terrible shrieks, almost inhuman, rise above all other sounds, but only the noise of crackling timbers and breaking slates was audible. At last, the smoke became so concentrated that the whole building erupted in flames.

As if the inferno was reaching out from the house and into my very being, I felt something inside being destroyed, and I cursed my own weakness. Courage can't be destroyed, I'd always thought. But this most recent event, in which my new model of bravery and all it meant was being burned up before my eyes, showed how courage could indeed be destroyed. And up with that went hope. I was left staring into a black hole of disgust and horror. And, worse still, despair.

All I could do was watch from a safe distance. As the coloured tongues rose to their climax and snapped at the underside of a blanket of black smoke, the shroud of evil spread to fill the afternoon air.

I wished fervently that Miss Antwerp had in her final moments drawn solace from fleeting memories — of that glorious April back in 1918 when she and Mylie had first got together, and it appeared as if they'd fallen through a hole in the earth at the far side of a field; or that night of the dance in the loft when she'd popped her head up from behind the bundle of hay to lay claim to a certain item of clothing. And once more it struck me that, with pain or joy ever dancing attendance, the business of recreation was all bound up with that of dying.

But more than anything else, I wished she could hear again the sound of a piano and tenor voice. Away in the distance at first, then through the middle of the endless black terror, the voice might come to soothe her. For it seemed at this moment that the song was meant for her alone.

Oh! Make her a grave where the sun-
beams rest,
When they promise a glorious morrow;
They'll shine o'er her sleep, like a smile
from the west,
From her own loved island of sorrow!

16

Our company lay low in Killoughrim Wood, but as far as the Tans were concerned we might as well have taken ourselves to the opposite side of the globe. We heard reports that they'd spent a week searching and pillaging. When they couldn't find a trace of us, the enemy eased off their pursuit; they probably deemed that we had gone to ground or moved out of the area altogether; it was a relief to know they hadn't used dogs in the hunt. Despite the ever-lessening acreage owing to farmers' hunger for land, Killoughrim Wood was still huge, and we felt safe there among the trees.

Even the driving March winds and rain were chastened to swirl-breezes and tree drops, and little more than touched or impinged upon us once we got used to the incessant rush and sough of the heaving vaults above. Likewise on the calmest of days, this soft womb of a place still sighed and heaved like a mother turned banshee on a long-term keen for the loss of a baby the world had forgotten. As the year unfolded, this canopy of swaying leaves would bestow yet more shelter on wayfarers in hiding. Tree sap like snails at night had already begun to rise, while a thick rotting carpet of leaves hid the earth and muffled our footsteps. The carpet was everywhere, and covered everything not standing.

We had concealed our makeshift homes by interweaving leaves and twigs, and had lined the undersides with straw and hung canvas tarpaulins beneath, making our huts good and dry. Each dwelling was concealed by boughs and thorns within a thicket, to any would-be intruders in the forest it would appear to be no more than dense undergrowth within brush. The men had been detailed to spend the first few days on this task and then, under cover of dark, to pay visits to the straw-ricks of nearby farmers; so as well as being safe, we were as cosy as bugs in rugs.

With the huts finished, there was little to do other than lie low and remain with the unit. I instructed the men to rest up and be patient till it was safe to venture out again. But things didn't work like that; you cannot lay down rules for temperament: the next couple of days were long-drawn-out, tedious, and it was hard to settle. The men were as fidgety as children at bedtime and talked too loudly. In the end a stern order to remain quiet had to be issued. It wasn't easy to put a finger on the general pulse or understand the tendency to be twitchy. There was nothing much wrong with us physically; no one was wounded other than Jerry Tobin. But then an odd thing: the humour changed yet again.

It happened all at once: a complete swing of the mood pendulum. As soon as I'd issued the order to be quiet, a brooding lethargy came over the camp, and every action became tired. Time itself grew sluggish, as if the world's clock had slowed down by two-thirds, and essential things, like rising in the morning, the change of watch and even the boiling of water, took ever so long. You'd think we were feasting on those toadstools scattered about. On top of that, the perpetual state of dusk, with nowhere to go, little to occupy hands or minds, and military discipline seemed to press upon us like some midnight lethargy till I could swear we lost track of the hours, the days even.

More than likely — and more than we cared to realize — we were affected by what had happened to the Antwerps: belated shock, or the grey dreariness that shock brings on. Since soldiers are expected to be immune to affliction and demise, no man could permit himself the luxury of grieving or showing the least sense of loss or any emotion

— other than fury. In war he has to hold the line of fortitude and be stern alongside his comrades, even at the cost of living out his days growing bitter, becoming a vinegary old fellow with a face on him like a frosted turnip in a January drill, and seeing his offspring turn to ice every time he walks into the room. Who better than veterans of war to know as much, and that damn all can be done for them?

Mylie was the one most affected. What happened to Miss Antwerp and her father had brought a stupor over him; he went into himself altogether and said little. His sadness rubbed off especially on us, his friends, who accounted for most of the men there, bar Rutch Kelly and one or two of his cronies.

On the afternoon of the tragedy, I had waited round till the Tans had finished their work and driven away in their lorries. When I withdrew to the wood and told Mylie, he wouldn't believe me; he had to see for himself. We went to the pile, which was still burning, but couldn't get near the front door for the heat. Nonetheless, through the hours of waiting there, the truth grew on Mylie.

At one stage, a sudden fit of anger had overtaken him. Right or wrong, he wanted to set out for town after the Tans. He'd get their addresses, by force if necessary, do in every last bloody one of them in their beds and . . . Mylie was strong: it had taken a lot for me to fell him and pin him to the ground till he calmed enough to see sense.

Some time before daybreak water bleared his eyes, as sadness at last got the better of him, and he tilted the old man's hat down over his forehead. The glowing pyre, occasionally stoked by the night breeze, would throw a touch of amber across his pupils. I had edged myself round to take advantage of any available light and keep a close check on him. But, again, all I could do was sit there and watch, till tiredness eventually got the better of both of us.

We returned the next day, but still couldn't prise a way inside the hot shell.

Are you sure you saw them being forced into the house? Mylie asked. You weren't mistaken? Maybe herself and her father were put in a lorry on the offside and driven away. Are you sure of what you saw?

Certain, I said.

He put the eyes through me, looking for uncertainty, the least smidgin of doubt — or hope. If I'd been anything less than confident about what I had seen, he'd have noticed it right off. I stared him back, defying him to believe what he didn't want to, but Mylie had begun to turn in on himself.

The listlessness that shrouded him was upon us all; an indolence that rose from the floor of the wood and dropped from the slow-heaving canopy above and, to an even greater extent, seeped from within our memories of recent happenings. Yet, looking back from this point in my life, I'm inclined to deem that sluggishness to have been more a fold of the forest in which to heal and be cosseted by nature than a state of apathy or a wasted time. For days afterwards, Mylie rose from his makeshift bed only to answer the call of nature or pick at his food.

There was no shortage of food. Friends and family sympathetic to the cause would come at night to the edge of the forest — they were never allowed nearer — with the things we needed. Mylie's brother Will was our main carrier. He kept us going with cigarettes and the best of Corrigeen Lane poteen, potent stuff and, as ever, strictly for taking as a nightcap — some people said it was wasted on the massaging of greyhounds' limbs. There was more demand for spirits and cigarettes than food. As always, each man held his cigarette with the lit end turned in towards the palm of his hand, and as we sat around late into the night, smoking and talking, with the campfire long since flickered out, not one give-away glow would you see in the dark.

That much, at least, of the Volunteers' drill had been learned well.

Nothing would do Mylie then but to attend Miss Antwerp's funeral. He wasn't let, though. It was too much of a risk: the RIC were bound to be there, or have their spies placed among the mourners. When we enquired into it, we found out little about the arrangements, or indeed if there would be any obsequies other than a very private burial.

At one time the Antwerps had been Protestants, but had long since given up churchgoing. It was hard to know whether they'd bothered with any creed; the main churches didn't hold much sway with them. By throwing the eye to heaven or giving a quick smirk-and-a-huh whenever religion came up, Miss Antwerp had shown little respect for the swaggers of clergymen — neither for the flaky *crabbit-shavers* of her own persuasion nor the power-hungry young parvenus of ours, who seemed to be *devoted more to corporeal pecking order and class than the saving of souls* — her words.

It was all very well, though, to go on about men in dog collars or whatever, but it didn't do the Antwerps any good having nobody to give them the proper rites of burial. What has a body got at the end, if not a few prayers said over them and a decent funeral to send them on their way? To an ageing man for whom the value of ceremony grows clearer, all rites of passage — obsequies, baptisms and weddings alike — are important.

⋆ ⋆ ⋆

Weddings . . . It's only like yesterday since our big day — Lucy, you remember? It was an autumn morning — what is it about September? Not that there were many trappings to recall: a small affair by modern-day notions. But that didn't belie the magic. We both valued simplicity, and strict formality was essential for the majesty of ritual, the augustness of ceremony. And we sensed our marriage was more bound up in that ceremony than in the trimmings. Morning nuptials, it was, then. I yoked the tub-trap and went to the church in the village. We had a breakfast afterwards, simple, and then away with us to the Strand Hotel for a few days by the coast, before the business of getting on with our lives.

The sun shone the whole time we were there, and sparkled off the tops of the waves like diamonds. You remember? Miles upon miles of beach: such an amount of sand and expanse of sea for mountain people to take in. The size of the dark-blue creature, flat-backed and beating its tail along the shoreline! It had, through its unending beat, a calming effect on us two midgets — what we appeared to be, there on the edge of the universe. We were like children, and little need had we for things to do but play along the beach and embalm each other with attention, in bliss and a dulled remembrance that there was a wide world outside.

Then in the evenings you'd come alive, when the bank of mauve set low beyond the offing, as the great creature before us turned to sapphires and rubies and the dusk filled with rose-light. Once, you picked up two oyster shells from the water's purple-tinted edge, clacked them together and tossed them back to the ocean. I didn't ask — which I've often regretted — what you meant by that. Was it the sign of some pact or other you'd made with the evening star for the two of us, or just an impulsive thing? Then you splashed me with spray: a blessing, like my mother's big fingers used to splatter us from the holy-water font inside the porch each time we'd leave home in a ritual that was as solemn in its observance, and as sacred, as any high altar rite. Ah, but, Lucy Brien, you surely had your ways. Far-off days, those are now, too.

* * *

Funeral or no funeral, wherever it might be held, Mylie Byrne wasn't going to be let pay his respects there. Not only would he risk being caught, he'd make a suspect of each person seen talking to him. If quizzed while standing on a stool with a Tan rope round his neck, who's to say he could resist blabbing? And the enemy would come swarming after the rest of us again.

For much the same reason, I didn't get in touch with Hannah Jordan. It was too risky even to send a message, let alone call at her house. Along with the others of Cumann na mBan, her every move was more than likely being watched. And with that devil's curse of a spy her father employed, Bobby Doran, the woman would surely get pulled in for the least slip. Or had Bobby already mentioned her to the peelers? Maybe she was more in danger than I'd allowed. All of a sudden, I became anxious for her safety. So I sent two fellows who knew where she lived to check. But they reported back that nobody had answered the door, and there was no smoke from the chimney. I hoped they'd have met her; that she might want to come and take refuge with us in the forest — just a passing wish.

Indeed, I could've done with Miss Jordan's company, her wisdom. She had been part of that inner group of people I'd come to depend on, but who were at that moment all beyond my reach. Apart from Mylie, who was too demented to have a conversation with, Miss Jordan was the only other person I could turn to. She would've understood the pall of sadness that hung heavily on my brain and compressed the very air to the lungs. I'd have told her how Miss Antwerp's voice called out through the dark; how I would wake in a sweat, sitting bolt upright on my straw mattress, experiencing the sensation that everything round me was on fire, and she'd have understood. For wherever she was at that moment, Miss Jordan was very likely going through this identical ordeal, with the same horror, the same guilt on her mind for having involved Miss Antwerp in the first place.

The majesty of the trees would've helped to pacify her torment and suited her composure, while she would've understood better than anyone the legacy of the forest, and that we weren't the first people to shelter in it.

One hundred and twenty years earlier, just after the '98 Rebellion, James Corcoran and his group, the Babes in the Wood, had come here and made the place their home for almost five years before being nabbed by Redcoats. Some of our men, including my brother Ben, were nervous after dark. Local people had it that on certain nights Corcoran and his men would still ride out, on their way to attack the yeomanry patrol that had terrorized people locally. Did anything ever change?

Let's listen, says Rutch Kelly, we might hear their steeds. You'd think he was reading from a children's storybook. We might hear hoofs clipping through the undergrowth, says he — the fellow was getting as foppish as the gent I'd taken the car from.

But Corcoran and his men's days had been numbered. The most powerful weapon the British ever had in this land was trained on them, and their comings and goings were watched.

Aye, and there was no shortage of spies, either, this time round. Damned spies.

⋆ ⋆ ⋆

Maybe if I'd known you better then, Lucy, I could've left the forest, gone to town at night when it was safe and spoken to you about what was on my mind. Or, rather, the time spent with you would've helped me forget, and I'd have found my own poise again after a short spell in the stillness of your presence. Besides, the sharing of great secrets and talking things through was hardly to become our style during those few short years we would be together.

There was too much urgency about our ways to allow space for trivial things, the past or topics that weren't immediate. Was that an uncanny recognition that your time with us would be cut short? We didn't need to chit-chat endlessly on. And I never once referred to the calamity at Antwerps' or the lasting mark it had left on my mind. And though you would've heard about the burning, the news having probably reached you at work in the hospital the following day, you never mentioned it to me either. Not that there was anything unusual about not wanting to bring up the dreadful event; everybody knew of it, but nobody wanted to talk.

As with any tragedy that ever befell the Black Country, people subtly refrained from mentioning it in their daily conversations, and then only around the fire-places at night would the odd allusion be made. But such references and momentary remembrances never amounted to more than *oh, those poor people, the Antwerps*, as if further details defied words, or that by uttering them the speaker might arouse and return the tragedy to their midst, that ancient dread of unwittingly reciting some evil chant to resurrect demons from the pits of the damned. Whenever the superstitious straddled the shadows around a great open fire with their yarns, they could spread foreboding to crickets creaking in the hob, and the neighbours listening would go hush, as if there was safety in silence.

But few people understood the real value and solemnity of silence more than you and I did. We also passed this trait to our offspring: not one of them was known to carry stories in childhood, going to school or afterwards. And to this day Jem will not talk about any neighbour, good, bad or indifferent. At the best of times his words are few, and even then he concerns himself solely with matters of work. Sarah is not much different: she never tells me about herself, her work or her social life.

On the other hand, though, Sarah is certainly never short of queries when she arrives home to pay us a visit, about twice a week. The moment she walks in that door, with pleasantries quickly cast aside, it's like she's still living here and has only been away for an hour, as she plies me with her trademark list of questions.

As if to flout this directness, however, and to taunt her about her most recent curiosity, when it's Rutch Kelly she is asking me about I like to digress from her line of questioning and relate the account of past events my way. As a result I've been doling out this story in dribs and drabs over the last few weeks. And when the point comes in each session where my concentration wilts, all I need do is suddenly query her fresh interest in the Trouble Times for her to look at me blankly, end the probing and concern herself with some other topic. Sarah used to throw that same blank look whenever I questioned her when she was a young adult and still under my roof.

Recently, I saw another version of that blank look on her face. Our second-born marched into the kitchen one evening — we don't often see Martin back here — and without realizing I was in the corner beside the fire he began to rib her.

How's my little sister's love life progressing? says he. Have you set the date for the big day yet?

It was less a silence and more a mixed state of embarrassment and surprise that enveloped the room, the way a sudden mist swirls down from the hill to cover everything and lead mountain travellers off course. The accidental way in which a confidence was divulged, rather than the content, was what jolted us, and I felt for Sarah in such a quandary.

But Martin wasn't worried, though; he just went on to talk of something else. He's a hasty fellow who never stops to think before he opens his mouth, and it didn't cross his mind that he'd robbed Sarah of the chance to tell me in her own good time. Not only was this news fresh, it was good news to my ears; for she'd shown no inclination before to settle, though she has had her share of suitors. In her late twenties, it's about time a girl finds herself a husband.

17

Damned spies!

From the moment the two Dorans had been brought to the camp in Killoughrim Wood for us to guard, the men were uneasy, strange as sheep when a dog prowls nearby, and they'd murmur to each other rather than speak freely like before. So an extra guard was mounted. Even Mylie emerged from his mourning to say: The sooner this business is carried out, the better. With the stupor he was in, he was capable of doing the job himself, right away, without seeing out the proper course of justice.

Having passed sentence, our local Republican court had allowed the prisoners a week to appeal — a bit lenient, but then our system of justice was only new — in which time they could come up with evidence either to mitigate the sentence or disprove the charge of spying. We were instructed to give reasonable scope and help, if they needed it — by heaven, I knew the help I'd give them. But neither man was taking advantage of his leeway to appeal. All they did was sit there and protest their innocence.

Any time I went near him, Tommy Doran would fix his eyes on me; as if staring at me was going to work for him. Blamed me, he did, because I was the one who'd seen him fire on Jerry Tobin!

I'm not a spy, says he. I'm the best soldier you have in this company, and well you know it.

Then why did you shoot Jerry Tobin? says I.

I didn't shoot him.

I saw you pointing the rifle.

It wasn't pointed at him! I was about to fire over his head to warn him off the road.

You almost killed that man. In fact, he might not recover from your bullet.

It wasn't my bullet, he'd shout.

To keep the Doran brothers safe while in our midst was enough of a strain without having to put up with their guff as well. My anger had been replaced by a cold hatred; I despised the sight of them, their smell and their least sound, and each time I thought of the Antwerps I had to stop myself from finishing them; were it not that some form of rectitude and show of discipline had to be upheld, I would've. I was even annoyed for allowing myself to get caught up in conversation with one of them — and afraid I might lose the run of my restraint.

Do you think I'm blind? says I. Do you suppose I didn't see your brother bring a letter to the loyalist in town, who went straight to the barracks with it; that I didn't follow him inside and spot the letter being handed over to the peeler on duty at the counter? No, I didn't see any of it — I bloody well dreamt it up. Mister, you were the first link in the spy ring. You passed on information to your brother, who then brought it to the Orangeman, the third link. All this has been thrashed out before the court, and the court has found you guilty. Now, either find something new to overturn the sentence, or shut up and wait for your execution.

I was the one who'd made the charge against the two Dorans. On our first day in the woods, though, I hadn't meant it to be such: I'd jotted down an account of how our attempts to attack must've been foiled by the passing of information to the enemy, that I had seen Tommy Doran shoot Jerry Tobin, and followed the trail of the envelope from the hands of his brother to the RIC barracks. I'd sent a copy of my notes to the captains of the other local companies. By evening the Dorans were on trial.

The two boys trudged slowly through the leaves along the main path. They were out on their walk: part of a scheduled exercise. It was more a way of keeping them warm than anything else — we didn't want them to freeze to death on us. Not that this would matter to them for much longer: where they were going, they'd have all the heat they needed.

Hands tied behind their backs and ankles fettered like mountain sheep on pasture, one followed the other. They were beyond being human: jute bags over their heads, with three yards of halter rope dangling from one neck to the other. While we couldn't take our eyes off them, it was hard to look on the creatures as anything other than farm stock, condemned farm stock, diseased, soon to be put down.

We'd do it humanely, though, and quickly. It grieves me to this day to see a creature suffer. But while no living thing ought to be let linger in pain, I'm reluctant to take the life of even the smallest insect; preferring to open a sash and let it fly out the window than splat its body against the glass. Life is that precious. But once the creature is diseased, is it not more humane to put it out of its misery?

I had been fond of Bobby Doran once, having met him when he'd chaperoned Hannah Jordan to night class in town, and got to know him better when he'd accompanied her to the anti-conscription meetings of 1918. But had he really punctured his wheel going to our first gathering, or had there been something more insidious behind his reason for letting our entire group pass before he'd approach where the peelers stood in that village?

Light-hearted and funny, he hadn't shown an interest in politics, one way or the other. And no man I knew had such a store of jokes: he never repeated the same one. Amenable though he was, what I'd admired most was his dependable nature: he'd always done his boss's bidding to wait for Miss Jordan. He had also widened the scope of my fondness for the lady; when you like the people who flutter round a person, it's natural to admire the person more.

There, at the butt of the tree, he lay like a small version of a ne'er-do-well you'd see skulking behind creels, or the *kanatt* in tow with each jobber at a Fair Day in town. When I tried to talk to him, he'd only curl up more, shiver and say: Find Miss Jordan. Please get Miss Jordan.

It was hard to see what Hannah Jordan could do for him. I again sent somebody to look for her — during the day this time, at greater risk. The word he brought back was:

she's gone to stay with her relations up the country, herself and her father.

His brother, Tommy, was an odd fellow. I'd been less fond of him, at least in the beginning, and found him hard to trust, for he'd been in the British Army. Because he'd befriended Rutch Kelly, too, it didn't help. But as time passed, and he'd put the men through their paces, shown how he could handle himself during an operation and demonstrated his skill with explosives, I had come to respect him. Worse still, I'd grown to trust him. It was not a begrudging kind of trust, either; I just naturally came to rely on him without question — even more so, at times, than on Mylie Byrne. I'd have put my life in that fellow's hands. Would have? I *did*. I'd put all our lives in his hands.

I wanted to know why he'd done it. Was it the money? Had he been sent to our locality, or decided off his own bat to join us and then turned . . . traitor — that most despicable word? If he'd joined with the best of intentions, and then changed his allegiance, you'd wonder what drove him to it.

Had he been in touch with the peelers when they'd travelled the far road to keep an eye on us: the times I'd spotted something — a mirror, possibly? By then, probably, he was regularly feeding them information about our patterns of drill. Since he'd been in on the planning of each operation, the peelers would have had our names, numbers, sizes and addresses; they'd have known all about us. They'd waited till we became organized enough to launch a decent ambush, and then they'd nab us — for didn't they damn nearly succeed?

And to think that we'd been about to include Tommy Doran in making the dugouts in preparation for the ambush below at the bridge. I can still feel sweat along my spine, can still picture it: the hatch being prised up, flung back from over our heads, and us staring into the barrels of half a dozen rifles. To meet those Tans' eyes and revolvers pointing, with no such thing as surrender, 'twould have been a matter of *goodnight, nurse, and kiss the baby*. Then, later, their voices would give an earful to some unfortunate innkeeper.

Like shooting vermin down their hole, it was. And if you don't put your best spirits on the counter before us — well, see that pistol there? — I'll put as many holes in your head, you old Fenian git, so be quick about it.

* * *

The usual forest sounds seemed to die off, allowing the traipsing rustle through the leaves to be clearly heard. Here he was, the final messenger. Even the birds of spring quietened for news. Along the path, he came, up towards us. He had a letter in his hand. Final word; it had to be read.

I'd expected as much, and had gone over in my head many times how to carry it out. The best way was to run it like drill practice: an order to be obeyed, no more. We'd wait till dark, of course. Not to be inhumane, the two of them would have to be done together. We'd bring them to a field gate by a road close to the village, so they'd be found by mid-morning. I knew the spot. A Croppy rebel had been hanged there back in 1798.

Two for the price of one? Scarcely fair appeasement: the value of a Croppy, a good Irish rebel, when weighed against a traitor's. Still, this offering should balance the reckoning and cancel the debt, and the forces of retribution need no longer dwell in the earth thereabouts to harangue the souls of passers-by. The idea of an eye for an eye — or two for one, when the two are inferior — is scarcely remarkable; when at war, a man must live by different regulations and the austere codes of ancient times are resurrected to enable a soldier to face his duty with clear conscience.

The two condemned creatures would be shown all due respect, treated with a dignity they hardly deserved. And maybe this effort at appeasement, the offering of itself, might, when added to their lifetimes' attributes and virtues, enhance their standing in some destined nether world. Still and all, I hoped they wouldn't notice the two pieces of cardboard under my coat ready to hang round their necks. I'd already written the standard message on each: SPY. ALL INFORMERS BEWARE. WE ARE ON TO YOU — IRA.

⋆ ⋆ ⋆

As darkness fell, the prisoners were sent ahead, guarded by four men. I brought Rutch Kelly with me, having thought about Mylie, but he had enough on his mind. Anyway, why not let Kelly take his share of the onus; see if he had the nerve for it. I carried two short arms in a belt hidden under my coat: the gun I'd hand Kelly had only one round — just in case. Neither he nor I opened our mouths as we walked there.

Myself and Kelly took charge of the prisoners, and the men who'd been guarding them were posted two hundred yards in each direction to block the road. Kelly carried the lamp, and the prisoners were led from the field, to the other side of the gate and onto the road.

The procedure began with the firm closing of the gate, shouldering it over the last clump of earth to smack it tight against the striking post, before dropping it into its home rut.

Slowly and in silence, we went through the rest of the routine. I blindfolded each of them, told them to kneel down and say their last prayers, took the lamp from Kelly and placed it on the hanging post of the gate. The shadows shook only for a moment. All other matters, final requests and what-have-yous had already been taken care of. I took the revolvers from my belt, handed one to Kelly and nodded him in the direction of Bobby Doran. I held the muzzle of my own Smith and Wesson a few inches from the temple of the other brother.

The prayers ended.

Bobby Doran spoke with a quiver in his voice: Why don't you ask Miss Jordan about the letter, and —

He said no more. The gun in Kelly's hand whip-cracked through the night's quiet, away beyond our cocoon of light and into the timeless dark. The ease with which Kelly carried out his task would unnerve you.

Since the two prisoners ought to be done together, without interval, I fixed my mind on a woman and her father being burned, their shrieks drowned out by the crackle of flame through that great tinderbox of a home.

A second crack split the night.

There was an instant unmistakable thrill, I must admit, as the warm flush of blood through my veins replaced the sickening dread I'd held for this business. Kelly felt the same — I caught sight of it in his face.

We tucked them up neatly to sit back against the gate: arms around the second rail up and hands in coat pockets to keep them from slumping forward. We straightened collars and dusted bits of straw from their shoulders. As if to keep the rest of the night's chill at bay, their caps, which had fallen off, we placed back on — the Dorans had always been great ones for caps. They looked, for all the world, like two drunks sleeping it off in a town doorway, towards the end of a St Thomas's Fair Day — the last fair before Christmas.

I hung the cardboard notices from their necks. All was done.

18

The turmoil across the land continued through the spring and summer, till the British Prime Minister, Lloyd George, finally realized it wasn't a gang of hoodlums and murderers he had to deal with in Ireland but a whole movement of people determined to govern themselves. The Tan War suddenly ended with the Truce in July '21.

But for many soldiers of the Irish Republican Army, this Truce had come too suddenly; the war had ended without rhyme or reason or a chance to wind down, and no intervening period was allowed for us to adjust back to civilian life. At least we were free to leave the forest.

Of all the happenings during the Troubles, the period we spent in Killoughrim Wood was what had the greatest effect on our company. The place had somehow established an odd, primal hold over us, with nobody anxious to depart from its folds, and the thought of walking out into the open again was almost frightening. When my turn came, it felt like I was being stripped naked in front of a crowd of leering peephole-gawpers as I stepped out into the clearing, through the fields and away. You could tell by their hesitant steps that the rest of the company felt the same; all, that is, except Rutch Kelly. He danced out under that July sun like a butterfly flitting towards a field of thistle-tops.

The forest had also been a place of forgetfulness. Once we had come to terms — except for Mylie — with the loss of the Antwerps, all other dire states of mind were ever on the outside of that basilica-like haven. And how relieved I'd been, too, not to have had guilt, remorse and despair as permanent attendants; nor was I burdened, either, by a weighty compunction after doing what'd had to be done to the Dorans. Instead, I'd experienced a certain satisfaction — and not just the temporary kick from a first-time killing; though that too — in believing I had rid the country of two traitors, making the possibility of another treacherous incident, like what'd befallen the Antwerps, less likely to happen. By executing those two, I knew I'd saved the life of many another, more worthwhile individual.

We'd got word of the Truce the day after it was signed. Mylie's brother Will had led a messenger from town into the forest, beyond the bounds of where anyone was allowed, when one of our look-outs spotted them.

Despite our company's lethargy, we had managed to plan and train for incursions and enemy exploitation of a messenger, like Will Byrne, as a ruse to find us. Almost within a minute of giving them the order, the men were back to being as sharp as feral cats, mobilized and in formation; within another three minutes, we were in position to deal with the intruders and to fall upon the enemy unit in pursuit. That's how well we'd adapted to surviving in the forest. The messenger carried written orders notifying us of the agreement and commanding us to cease all engagement with the enemy. Still concerned in case this was a ploy, I waited till nightfall and sent men to the other local companies to find out what was happening.

Even when we'd received confirmation of the cease-fire and the order that the company was to be temporarily stood down, the men were reluctant to leave the twilight of the great dome, and then only stole away in dribs and drabs back to their families. Each man hesitated, as if he was wary of breaking a bond he'd made with the trees to keep them company and to safeguard them from encroaching farmers, while in return the forest hid him, and sheltered him from the elements and from being pestered by demons to both body and mind. Or maybe he dithered because he was sorry to leave that primeval place.

* * *

We'd made it through the Troubles, and seen the end of the British — off they went, at least from this part of the island, tails in the air, like cattle over a brow, to fresh pastures. Then we had a year's break from strife, nearly, in which to try and live normal lives, before the other thing started: the abomination. To this very day the mention of its name brings on a spate of deliberate amnesia; heads drop, conversation, which was lively up to now, fizzles out and caps are donned. Nobody wants to talk about that conflict, or name people.

The Civil War broke out in June '22 and lasted till May '23. Short though it was in one way, in another it seemed to have neither beginning nor end, and haunts us even today. It still puts lead in our step, the same as how the '98 Rising affected our forefathers all through the nineteenth century, and holds back a race of people. The vilest of conflicts, surely, was that of Cain against Abel.

It would be nice to say I'd got involved in the Civil War out of principle; that I'd weighed up the Anglo-Irish Treaty, the issues of partition, with the likes of Hannah Jordan there — where had she disappeared to, near the end of the Tan War? — and then come to my own conclusions. Of course there were debates; was anything else ever talked about during the lull between the two conflicts?

Though nobody wanted hostilities, they were bound to happen, as opposing beliefs hardened. One side of the debate saw partition as a stepping-stone towards the final goal of thirty-two counties, and believed that the British — whose hands were tied by northern Loyalists — wouldn't budge on their offer. The other side argued that Ireland was one nation, couldn't be divided and the fight must go on; it was all or nothing. And in the only language the old foe understood, we'd convince them to raise their offer from twenty-six to thirty-two. After seven centuries of domination by a foreign people and government, were we to be given back — have thrown at us, more like — three-quarters of what was ours? Had we even the right — a birthright sanctified by sacrifice, with the precious stain of the 1916 Easter rebels little more than dry — to take such an offer? And how could we accept in the name of the dead generations and exiled children a deal that isolated our brothers in the North? Such were the arguments of my fellow soldiers; not necessarily mine.

None of those debates or meetings that I attended helped me to come to any definite point of view. As the year passed, the arguments became heated and people's tempers boiled over till all hope of avoiding another bloody war disappeared.

The rights and wrongs of each cause aside, I just didn't have the stomach for further bloodletting, certainly not that of friends and brothers. But this monster of a thing stole up on me. The fact is — for what has an old man got, if not some truth with himself? — I decided to wait till Rutch Kelly showed his hand first, and then I'd make up my mind. Whichever side he'd take, I'd take the other; no need to bother with issues.

From the early days, when he'd been out of control, the man was the lodestar to set a course by. To even the greatest of idealists, the rule of thumb was simple: oppose the likes of Rutch Kelly in everything; decry what he got up to and a fellow wouldn't go wrong — except of course in singing.

He joined the Free State army, the Regulars — they must've had more perks to offer him than their opponents. To see the man strut cock-of-the-walk through the village in his uniform — high-collared tunic, five buttons down the front and one on each pocket lapel — was like watching, all but for the missing handlebar moustache, an English major who'd forgotten to pull out alongside his troops after their occupation, and in need of being brought down a peg or two. So I joined the Irregulars, simple as that, as did most of the men from my old company. For us it was a case of back to former duties, the drill and the fear of not making it through this time, maybe even of not making it past our next engagement; or worse still: the dread of wounds that permanently injure, and to end up a gimp for the rest of your days. As one enemy replaced another, it was a return to ways that appeared even more ghastly than before: a soldier had been much less aware the first time round. And it was easier to fire on a stranger than on somebody you knew, even if that somebody was the like of Rutch Kelly.

From the start, our side controlled the county towns and surrounding villages. But the advantage didn't last long. We couldn't hold out against the regular army; with their field guns and heavy-duty weapons, they swept down through the centre of the county. We had nothing to match such firepower, and the village my unit had been sent to help defend fell quickly to the enemy. The machine-guns rattled enfilades at our cover and laced our men to the floor, not allowing us to take up proper firing points. And on top of that the enemy lined up their field gun to blast at our more entrenched points. To save the men's lives, I saw no choice but to surrender.

According to their positions, however, the majority of our soldiers managed to escape; many were wounded, while a few were killed. The rest of us were captured, bundled into a lorry and brought to the station; then we were loaded onto the Dublin train for internment camp throughout the rest of the war.

Our journey had little more than begun when the train was attacked and stopped outside the main county-town. Panic spread along the carriages like fire through a tinder-box, and we dropped to the floor. Owing to lack of space, and being one of the last to be loaded, I'd been located at one end of a guard's carriage, away from the main prisoner group. With the aid of a sharp metal seat-prop, I was able to undo my wrists. The train moved on again. A guard came through and turned to lock the door behind him, but before he got a chance I downed him, took his revolver and jumped off. I was spotted. Shots were fired from the moving train and I got hit in the thigh. Still, I'd managed to escape.

The Irregulars who'd attacked the train picked me up and hoisted me away to safety, and I ended up in the same ward of the infirmary as Jerry Tobin had over a year before. It was reckoned that once the doctor removed the bullet, I should leave: the Regulars would come for me. Though needing to recuperate, I couldn't very well go home: it was the first place they'd search. So two of the nurses, who were members of Cumann na mBan, moved me to a storeroom, behind a stack of mattresses, and the door was kept locked. Those furies of women ran that establishment like they owned it.

And that's where you came into the picture again, Lucy Brien. You took my mind off all fighting: the excitement of waiting to see you replaced the expectation of battle-cry, and I experienced a new stimulation altogether different from the thrill of a scrap, or the feel of the kill. The warmth of your hand replaced the touch of a tender trigger against my finger — such sudden change, though, brought a shock that took getting used to. The peace you brought turned me against conflict. It was like a punishment, then, leaving your softness to go back to fighting.

When I joined the lads again, what was left of our old company, they were on the run from the Regular army, sleeping in safe houses and hay sheds by day and then on the move throughout the night. Still, we managed to attack the odd depot, under cover of darkness, and to set on fire a few estate houses where the enemy had set up garrisons and depots — the ruins of which are standing to this day. But our side was weakening throughout the country. A truce was called in May, and the fighting stopped: that much, at least, of the Civil War had ended. Thank heaven. It was not a conflict I care to remember, or one in which I ever took pride in having participated.

Your presence, Lucy, removed my will for a good scrap, the need to feel that rush of blood or stand over a body squirming in its last throes. Brought me peace, you did. And I'm ever grateful.

But you're no longer here . . . other than a spectre in my head, a shade to one side of my eye in the kitchen of a September dusk. Must a mottled old man make do with the old longings?

19

Yet still I long for September evenings when dusk lingers and there are no severe borders between shade and light, or between the present and the past recalled. At such times, memories become as real as the here-and-now, almost. It's as if life can be breathed into the faces on a frayed-edged photo any time it is taken out of a wallet, and the lost moment that the snap once distilled can be restored. For the world of the past becomes reinstated here in the kitchen twilight, across the floor, on the chairs and even in shapes the burning *greesach* makes on the hearth. And I can see my old pal again — and old pals are ever the best — alongside his dear friend.

The lord and lady of the manor are standing on the porch of their large, pleasingly shaped house, and with wheels ploughing ruts through the pebbles I hoot and steer my Model T motorcar up the driveway that curves too much. With his thumb, Squire Byrne flicks up the hat to scratch his forehead, while his other arm tugs on the lady's shoulder. The genial hostess beckons me in for tea. I don't mind if I do, says I. What-ho, perhaps so.

And a touch of croquet on the lawn then? asks she.

I'd love a touch of croquet, Mylie says with a grin.

That was the last time I saw so carefree a grin — blithe beyond a smidgin of human worry — on his face, the last mental snap I have of Mylie Byrne when he was himself.

He never fully got over the death of Miss Antwerp. During the lull in the Troubles and for years afterwards, we tried to keep Mylie from withdrawing into himself. Most evenings after work, myself or Ben, or one of his other old friends, would go up the lane to his house and insist on taking him to Murphy's in the village for a few balls of malt, and we regularly brought him to the supper-dances in town, of a Wednesday or Friday night.

Though he soon got back on track in the natural way he had with the ladies, especially the older ones, a certain callousness — beyond the apathy that comes from constant prowess in the field — had infected his charm, which of course only made him more alluring to the species. One of the lads remarked: Mylie Byrne's grown into a heartless devil. But he didn't know the circumstances. Mylie never got caught up with another woman. Instead he took a shine to all women, one after the other each night, a walking Venus flytrap for females.

Eventually, the bloody old consumption got the better of him, and he took to bed with weakness. One evening towards the fall of year, when I called to see him, Mylie asked me to do him a favour. He wanted me to bring him a woman, one of his sweethearts from town.

Damn it, your mother will kill me if I bring you a fancy woman here, says I.

Don't come while my mother's in the house, says he. What's wrong with you? Bring her here next Sunday morning while my mother's at Mass and I'll be on my own.

I made arrangements with the girl he asked for, and brought her along: in through the front porch — nobody there — up the stairs with us, to the room. As I walked out again and closed the door on them, Mylie winked; his old grin had almost returned as he saluted and spoke his last words to me.

Aye, Captain! I will now proceed to carry out my duties like any decent soldier in the army of the Irish Republic should, and I'll march down the road all good rebels go.

By the time I'd reached the bottom step of the stairs, the weight of himself and Miss Mags Brophy made the bed creak overhead like the whole shebang was about to collapse through the ceiling before I could take myself outside.

Three days later, of a Wednesday in the autumn of the year 1934, Mylie's heart stopped.

* * *

In the twilight of an early September evening, the picture of another old friend regularly comes to mind. An attractive creature, she was too, with such elegant poise to her movements, and she once held my affections in her hand like she was the sole damsel of the area, the only girl from here to Ballyanne. For quite a while, had she but shown the slightest romantic interest in return, things might've turned out an awful lot different. You can never forget dreams of what might've been, or the times in which dreams were forged, when you didn't doubt that such foolish imaginings would come to pass. Ah, well. As age catches up, you dream back, never forward.

She once had such lovely light, not quite red, hair parted off-centre, high cheekbones and a high forehead — a huge capacity for brains. A complexion, too, for the summer sun; by September the freckles on her face and wrists were as bronzed as burnished gold

— at least, memory makes them so. I recall her keenness for the Irish language and her ideas of nationhood. How she used to frown at my thinking that national independence was an end in itself, my simple and straightforward aim. She had a bigger picture: the revival of the language, traditions, culture and learning — where real freedom lay — and political independence was but one part of that. I was taken by her grand notions, or was it the way she said them, and the shape of her mouth? But as for the chance of a court off her, the blinds were down. I never managed to get my hands round her torso for the least *hoult*. And that's what had me confused at first.

She was interested enough to travel with me round the county to all those anti-conscription meetings of 1918. She used her membership of Cumann na mBan and influence, in quarters unknown to me, to help with my preparations for ambushes against the Tans. Yet she never let me near her.

What Miss Antwerp had said about her friend, the night of the dance in the loft, had given the game away. Hannah Jordan was a little bit peculiar, more interested in the girls than the boys. I'd heard of suchlike before, women or men who were only attracted to their own kind, but I was never formally introduced to one. While it was difficult to fathom such leanings, I managed, just about, to reason away my bias towards Miss Jordan's predicament. And even though little could be done to rearrange her pickle, this weakness of birth, it was easy to be tolerant of her. The lady had so many other qualities it was hard to blame her for one little bend in the rope. The fact that her friend Miss Antwerp could be so jocular and direct about her own tastes helped to take away any harm, and make the matter unimportant, almost funny — as long as the lads didn't hear about it.

I'll not make flesh of one and fish of another, Miss Antwerp once remarked. She wasn't the least bit shy in joking about her leanings. Maybe it's gone like what's happening nowadays with Fridays — a person can eat either fish or meat — that in the end it makes no damned odds which one is chosen; it's all a question of taste.

But if Hannah Jordan wouldn't let me near her, why did she turn round and go consorting with his nibs, Rutch Kelly, and then marry him? How could she lie down and baby-make with him, while such actions ran against her inclinations? The woman managed to confound me totally.

But, of course, now I know why. It took me years to figure it out, though the answer is simple. Money is why, or land — the same thing. If property can change the high-mindedness of the noblest gentry, why should Hannah Jordan be any different? By such reckoning she, too, was entitled to forgo her ideals and odd preferences, and end up poking about in Rutch Kelly's codpiece, all in the interests of convenience or gain. All ideals aside, isn't everything about shillings and status? (Her standing would later be enhanced when one of their children became a doctor.) And land — especially land, at the end of the day.

* * *

Not long after her marriage, I came across Hannah Jordan — bumped into her in town at Christmas time. She was loading purchases into her tub-trap down Main Street, opposite the church, and I offered to lift a bag of Pollard for her.

Thank you, Jim, says she meekly, the head down.

I asked her into the snug of the pub nearby for a drop of sherry to fortify her against the cold of the road home, and for old times' sake. But when she pulled her scarf up round her head, I became very unsettled. It wasn't the fact that she'd worn this same scarf, or one very like it, to our first protest meeting back in 1918; it was the colour: the way it reminded me of some untoward happening. My memory almost clicked, but the flash went too quickly. Wasn't it strange that I should feel queasy at the sight of the colour mauve?

Though Miss Jordan avoided my eyes, and it was obvious she was very ill at ease with me, she was willing to talk. And we chatted about the old days, before I said what was on my mind.

Will you tell me, how did you ever end up marrying Rutch Kelly?

Such a barefaced question made her perk up, as if she was about to rebuke me, but she settled for the safety of a slight haughtiness of old: an aloofness that once used to make her elegant, which I no longer found to be so alluring. It was an arranged marriage, says she. Her father had come to an agreement with Kelly's father through a middleman. Because the eldest Kelly would take over the farm, there was no room there for the bold Rutch. But the family would look after him. Yes, they'd find him a cosy little place, if not a decent-sized farm, to marry into, and so the matchmaker was called in. Now, Lucy, my girl, you remember what you once said about farmers and matchmaking? Well, there's no need to say I told you so.

Rutch's uncle, Pat the Hat — another Kelly — acted as middleman. No better people for keeping things nice and tight. His mission was to find a property whose owner had no sons and an only daughter. To say that Rutch fell on his feet is putting it mildly; there was no comparison between Jordan's place and the humble Kelly homestead. The luck of the devil!

No doubt marrying you improved his manners, I said.

I'm with child, says she. Doesn't that tell you? And she threw me a sore look, our first eye contact since we'd met outside on the street.

Once again I was willing to make allowances, even appreciate Miss Jordan's predicament, while I could no more understand her than the man in the moon. Then, acting on an impulse to reassure the lady, I placed my arm round her shoulder, and for a moment it was like the meeting of a long-lost brother and sister; but this odd, pleasant sense from the past quickly dissolved as she pulled away and her unease seemed to bob up again. And I ended up having to assure myself that whatever worm bothered her it was hardly there on my account: I'd tried to be nice to her, and genial. At once, I recalled a previous time, a similar situation — can you ever forget an incident, no matter how distant, which was full of qualms and suspicions? It had occurred during the picnic on our way to that protest march; with the sound of convivial delight drifting over the grass from the far side, and with cordiality a lot less plentiful on our side of the field, I had failed then to read the situation, or to know where I stood with Miss Jordan. This time round, as old confusions returned, it seemed I was once again reading the circumstance of our meeting all wrong, and that somehow my presence was what really unsettled the woman, rather than her earlier state of mind.

Damn it, Hannah Jordan was just too complicated a character for me. And yet, in realizing as much, it seemed I was beginning to come to terms with my own likes and tastes. I had learned a lot from that woman.

⋆ ⋆ ⋆

I met her on another occasion, a year or so later. This time it was surprising, and sad, to see how she'd lost so much of her old vitality and looks, and was ageing beyond her time.

Before you ask, says she, I'm with child again. I'm thinking marriage is not the state that best suits me.

Well, beat that for news!

20

I have to put this dreaming on hold till I see who's driving into the yard. The vehicle, more like a sputnik than a motorcar, has stopped and the engine is switched off, yet the two people are slow to come out. Who can they be?

The passenger door opens first. With one foot suspended, and then the other, like she's a film star, the lady slews round on the seat, and gradually it is Sarah who emerges. But who is the driver — another film star? The driver's door opens; it's some young man I don't know. Sarah goes round, links his arm and leads him up to the house. I'm glad for her, at last, but I must hold my composure and remain somewhat aloof — how would Hannah Jordan manage to do it?

Daddy, this is Richard Kelly, says she.

If she's nervous, it doesn't show. He's a tall, fine-looking and pleasant young man, though he might maybe do with putting on a little meat. Indeed, you could mistake them both for a pair of film stars. But what is it about that name? No, it's probably a coincidence. How good it is to see young people happy, especially when one of them is your offspring. That daughter of ours would lighten the gloom of a tomb when she smiles. This is truly a good day.

There's no doubt but that he's fond of her. He'd better be. He has a face like someone I know — again, coincidence, I'm sure. He certainly has the cut of money about him — look at that two-seater sports car! Mind you, it wouldn't carry many sheep to the mart. Which reminds me: I must get on to Jem to buy a better jalopy than the one he has. It might help to take him out of himself, and to get to know a few women — a business that son of ours could do with attending to; the effort used to acquire a little female friendship would pay him better than spending all his time with mountain hoggets and rabbits.

I hope this fellow can support Sarah, but I mustn't marry them off just yet. She'd never have invited him here, though, if they weren't serious; he's the first lad she's brought home for me to inspect. And no better man to carry out an inspection.

What do you do for a living, Richard?

I'm in the medical profession.

Whereabouts are you in it?

But Sarah cuts in before the lad can answer. Daddy, Richard is a psychiatrist.

Where?

I'm a doctor in the mental hospital.

Well, bloody fecking hell. At last the penny drops; the pieces are beginning to fall into place, as they say. So that's what has been behind Sarah's questions and her recent interest in history — or, rather, her keenness for the family history of certain people. Didn't I know there was something behind it? And now like all things must, it has come out in the wash. But of all the doctors in hospitals the wide bloody world over, she had to go and pick a son of —

Is Rutch Kelly your father's name?

It is.

It is; so it is. Now, Sarah, I'll tell you what you'll do with this psychiatrist doctor. You take this son of a hoor, this friend of yours, out the yard and away from here this minute, and don't let me see him here again or I won't be liable for my actions. Not under any circumstances will I have the offspring of a Kelly under my roof. Nor do I want him anywhere near a daughter of mine.

Sarah's face has gone red with shock, and her ire is beginning to rise. But what did she expect? She's been told enough about that lot over the last few weeks to know better than to darken my door with a Kelly.

She throws me that look again. Come on,

she calls him. And, head down, without turning to look me in the face, the lad duly follows her out the door. As if to point up her audacity, she links arms with him across the yard to the car. I know her defiance.

She'd hardly be related to you, Lucy, if she was anything but a bit rebellious. Nevertheless, she's a big girl now and ought to be able to take a little reproach from her father over such an indiscretion. And there's no need for you to be pointing a finger at me either; I'll have enough self-reproach in the twilight here to handle without your harassing me.

Who's to say what road Sarah will go down? But one thing is for sure, I'll not have a son of Rutch Kelly under my roof. You know that very well too, Lucy Brien.

⋆ ⋆ ⋆

Shem, the postman, rides into the yard on his Honda 50. I suppose he expects some tea, as usual. He hands me a few letters, which I leave on the shelf of the dresser, not wishing to open them while he's here, and he realizes that. But one of the envelopes holds my attention, and his experienced beady eye combined with a nose for gossip-fodder notices such a distraction.

Like he's here on a holiday, Slurpy Shem

sips his tea and nibbles at a slice of bread, and with eyes zipping between me and the dresser he is all but asking, if not actually daring, me to violate the seal and breach the privacy entrusted in me by the sender. Wouldn't he just love to know what's inside that coloured envelope — and wouldn't I?

It's three weeks ago now, says he.

Three weeks since what? I ask him.

Since the day you had the grand car in the yard.

Not only is this postman of ours a nosy busybody, he must also be keeping a diary. It'll be interesting to see how much he knows, or if he's just fishing for tidbits. Somehow he has made a connection between that one envelope and the sports car. I'll have to be careful not to let him see I'm more distracted than he's already detected — for Sarah hasn't put in an appearance here since, and that's not like her.

Yeah, I was thinking of getting a car like that for myself, I tell him. It would be nice to drive to town in, of a Friday, and bring home the meat for Sunday. And I'd lend it to Jem the odd time for going to the mart; he'd surely carry a dozen lambs in it.

A nice car, right enough, says he, but it's maybe a bit flash for your needs. Sarah and her new man passed me the day they were here, driving like it was a rocket they had under them.

Travelling fast, were they?

All I saw was a flash going by me.

So, how did you recognize them?

The snap at him belies a brusqueness I've failed to keep under rein; it means I'm not so taken with this game as I might've liked, and maybe he ought to be on his way; for I'm closer to my wits' end than I've realized. Though oftentimes I indulge him, and play along with his sort of codology, this occasion is not going to be one of them.

Shem gets the message, finishes his tea and rises to go. Anyway, it's time he was back straddle-legged on his own little red rocket and out the yard with himself.

Now for that coloured envelope in peace, and I'll use a knife rather than tear it open. Mylie Byrne's dagger is still in the drawer of the dresser: he told me to take it as a keepsake following that fight long ago with Rutch Kelly over the leadership of the company.

'Dear Mr Rowe,' the letter begins — and a very proper beginning too. 'It appears that my son Richard has formed a friendship with your daughter, Sarah. He has told me you are unhappy with their liaison. In fact, I'm none too pleased about it either. It seems at least we have that much in common. If my husband and I were to get together with you, perhaps we could discuss the matter further to see if anything can be done to resolve the quandary. May I suggest we meet in town, in the Corner House Hotel next Friday at 4.00 p.m. [Signed] Hannah Kelly.'

It's not what she says, or the tone of her letter, that bothers me, and I have no qualms about meeting those two, either separately or together. There is something else. The handwriting; I've seen it before. It's so very precise, almost perfect, as if printed rather than done by hand. Is it not very like the written list that we found during the raid on the barracks long ago? And together with the envelope that contained it — how I've come to abhor the colour mauve.

It can't have been . . .

I remember the strict, almost severe, lettering of the register of all the names in our company, from Rutch Kelly to Mylie Byrne, without a word spelt wrong, and where my name was on the very first line. How can a person forget a hand that is draped in treachery? Addressed to the Officer in Charge, Crimes Special Branch, at the RIC Barracks, the mauve envelope we found it in was sealed inside a larger brown one. As neither envelope had been stamped, the letter had obviously been delivered there in person. Following the raid, I gave it to my brother Ben, ordering him to guard it with his life, and he still has the letter: only recently, he asked me to take it or he'd have to burn such an unholy relic. He said it was troubling him more as he got older to have an evil amulet like that in the house. I was about to tell him to do what he liked, but I thought better of it and, instead, said I'd take the thing off his hands.

I'll walk down to Ben's house right away and check it with what the postman brought me this morning. Anyway, I need somebody to talk this over with. There was a time when I'd have gone straight to Hannah Jordan with my predicament. Now, of course, she's the one person I cannot approach.

⋆ ⋆ ⋆

Ben looks at me intently when I ask him for it, and without a word he opens a drawer of the dresser, his filing cabinet, and from underneath a bundle of papers he pulls out a faded brown envelope and hands it to me.

He was right; there is a cold, unholy touch to it, and I open it quickly to compare the address on the faded-mauve envelope with the writing on the list inside. Ben watches me closely as I then take out of my pocket the letter I got from Hannah Jordan this morning. Though the latest script here is slightly less exact, a little shaky from age, there's no mistaking the hand. The one person wrote everything.

What's wrong with you? says Ben. Here's a drop of poteen, the best Corrigeen Lane brew; great for muscle and bone, and for rubbing into greyhounds — but wasted on them nevertheless. He pulls out a large bottle of what appears to be water from the bottom of the dresser. You look like you need it.

I show him the list. Look at this, I tell him. And now compare it with the letter I brought with me.

What of it? he asks.

Do you notice anything about the writing?

More than likely, says he, they were written by the same person. So what does that mean?

It means that whoever wrote this letter is the person who gave our names to the peelers during the Troubles. She was the one who was informing on us. And it was she who brought the Tans after us the time they burned the two Antwerps.

Why do you say that?

This is the same colour envelope as the one that Bobby Doran handed to the loyalist merchant in town, who then brought it down to the barracks. Damn it, Ben, Bobby was simply doing what his employer's daughter had asked him to do: deliver a message . . .

21

The last time I walked these streets when there was the same weighty sense of something impending seems like only yesterday. Although many yesterdays have come and gone since, the various habits of shopkeepers and street dwellers never change, an awareness of which at this moment feels oddly reassuring. Ahead of ordeals with unpredictable outcomes it was ever the same: I would tend to look around for the comfort to be had from the permanence in things.

So once again I dally outside shops to absorb the mid-morning smell of bread, the flurry of business inside, and the skill of Will Byrne, the carpenter, who's so busy hanging a door he's probably no longer conscious of performance or of his part in the theatre of this street, 'cept for the odd scan round to see who's noticing him. And there's that old shop next door: the face and style of the proprietor's apron may have changed over the years, but you'd always know a butcher by his capers behind a meat counter. While tending to one, his eyes stray to weigh up the next woman, and the next, as he lines up apt quips from his hard-earned, well-remembered stash of customer charm assaults.

And how would you like your sausages today, Mrs Brien? With a bit of fat in them, or on the lean side? Sorry, Mrs Brien, I keep forgetting you were never one for the limp sausage.

Oh, you're a desperate man, Wally Furlong.

Riveted by what was always town life at its best — between mid-morning and lunchtime — I'm strolling the pavements on the look-out for further distraction, wishing that the afternoon would keep away or else that it would come and go as quickly as possible. As my fingers caress cold iron inside my coat pocket, I'm at once aware of its intimate familiarity, and the throbbing of my ear-drums, a much more recent intimacy, grows louder.

There's the shop where the loyalist merchant had his business, the fellow who took that letter — and how many more besides? — from Bobby Doran. But let me tell you, he was gone within the year; we called in to see him of a winter's evening when he was about to close shop and gave him a week to clear out, or else . . . But first we made him open the safe in his office at the back of the shop. We didn't touch his cash; we were after information, and that's what we came across.

In the loyalist's diary for 1921, a number of entries showed that he'd received letters by hand and had immediately passed them over to the RIC. The peelers had obviously kept him informed; for underneath each mention of having received a letter, he'd made a short reference note. There were three dates in particular that were of interest to myself and Mylie. The first two said: *Details of planned ambush on patrol*. And the third one said: *Location of rebel hideout*.

Mylie reacted badly to that third entry, and wanted to do your man on the spot. For the *location of the rebel hideout* had meant the betrayal of Miss Antwerp.

To give him something else to think about, I handed Mylie the diary and told him to go through it carefully at home and see which entries had corresponded with our activities over that period.

Now, Bobby Doran's voice during his last hours comes into my head; how he kept on asking for Hannah Jordan, because she was the one who'd sent him to the merchant with the mauve-coloured envelope. She was the one who could've saved him — now I know. I allow my hand to tighten on the iron in my pocket.

★ ★ ★

The last day I was talking to him, Ben admitted he wasn't all that surprised by the news: over the years, he'd heard rumours and the odd jibe, like *The Doran boys weren't given much of a chance to prove their innocence*, in Murphy's pub coming up to closing time. He'd once heard a woman chastise her child with *I'll give you the same chance Bobby and Tommy got*. She'd rattled off the warning jingle unaware of its origin or even that she was in the company of an old IRA man, while in vain her husband had been throwing her looks that could kill. The sorest cut had come, Ben said, in Murphy's one night as Patsy, the barman, watched him scrawl with the stub of a pencil on the back of a fag-box a few items of grocery he'd remembered.

It's a pity my two cousins weren't asked to write something down on paper, or they might be alive today.

There are those who yet maintain that the brothers could neither read nor write, Ben insisted to me.

They didn't have to read and write to be able to send messages, I said, when I recovered my poise. They could've employed somebody to write for them.

Ben looked at the envelopes and letters on the table. Who? says he: Hannah Jordan? And there were other rumours.

At once he hesitated, as if realizing he'd already said enough. But having started, he wasn't going to be let off the hook. What other rumours? I roared. And he studied me for a few seconds before relenting.

Rumours that Hannah Jordan had joined Cumann na mBan to gain access to information on the Republican movement and, wrapped round her little finger, you were wheedled into colluding with her to such an extent you used the Dorans as patsies and executed them before she could be accused of spying; in which case the same accusation might be laid at your door.

What tongue would spread poison the like of this? But, for the moment, I didn't want a name. So I shouted at him: That's enough! I couldn't bear to picture a face, or know anything about the person who'd uttered those words, for fear of my becoming as obsessed with such wrath of reprisal as Ben's eye-opener had prompted, and then to be laden down with an aftermath of attrition — at my age.

I wasn't going to tell Ben my ideas of what lay behind Hannah Jordan's treachery: how the social class she'd come from had supported Home Rule, to be attained by parliamentary means only; that her family was a well-off pro-British and bitterly anti-Republican crew; so it was easy to understand why she might've wanted to make a stand and had ended up spying against us — there could be little doubt any more but that the lady had been a spy. Yet, while she'd held political views that were distinct from mine, our opinions hadn't been that far apart, and we'd never really been at odds over our differences. Besides, I didn't believe she'd been an anti-Republican or that her actions were taken to advance the political ideals of family and class.

It's clear to me now how the sharp brain that lay behind Hannah Jordan's blue eyes was riven by something much more intimate and primal than politics. A streak of pure jealousy was what tore at the lady's insides, and sent her down the road to perdition. What had probably begun to affect her in a field back in 1918, when her dear friend, Miss Antwerp, took a shine to Mylie Byrne, gradually developed till it turned into a monster she could no longer control. It was the reason too for her aloofness, and why I could never really fathom her. But that was no cause for treachery, at least not of the kind she visited upon our heads.

I cannot let it be. Some sort of reckoning will have to show before this day is out. At last those two men may be given their say; for no one's voice, of either saint or demon, can be shut up for ever; it's against the run of nature.

Before walking in there, I need to stop and face the doorway, take out the Smith and Wesson and fill the chambers with a few crimped-end bullets, leftovers from training long ago.

⋆ ⋆ ⋆

It's well past four. So, let them wait. The girl at the reception says the Kelly family has the small function room at the head of the stairs booked for the evening. I'll give them function . . .

I open the door. Seated round a large table, they drink tea and pick at tidbits; a phoney set-up. Anyway, country people tend to become stiff inside hotels and town eating-houses, but this is beyond that. I could sense nervousness from halfway up the stairs: their fits of laughter were too strident. As I step into the room, the level of talking drops, then stops, and the dull rattle of delft increases rapidly. Is there no bone china to be had in these places any more? You'd miss its tinkle.

I know what I'm going to do, and it certainly isn't to stand like a *stookaun* inside the door, waiting for someone to ask me to join them; but first I must check who's present. Sarah sits beside her man — to be expected of course; I only wish the circumstances were different for them. Why is my son Martin here? He's with his wife. So it's meant to be a bloody social occasion, as well? We'll see.

Martin gestures to me to sit beside him, but I'm not here to sit.

Rutch Kelly seems to have aged certainly no more than at the normal rate of decline — even maybe a little less — and the young man beside him must be another of his offspring. A mottled old woman sits at the other side of Kelly. Heavens above, is that his wife?

The old one with the tortoise-shaped head: is that Hannah Jordan? I haven't laid eyes on her since she was carrying her second child; she was beginning to age then, but how can she have become so decrepit, stooped? She's ready to fall off the edge of that chair. She'll surely collapse at the sight of a Smith and Wesson. But I'm here on business, and I will not be sidetracked by an old woman's appearance, or by memories.

Come and join us, Rowe, and we'll have a

cup of tea, says Kelly. Or have something stronger, if you like. A drop of malt?

He's become mighty benevolent in his old age. I'll give him something stronger if he'd like!

I'm not here to sip tea, I tell him. And I put my hand in my pocket to feel for the revolver.

Oh, do sit down and have a cup of tea, my good man; we're all family now, nearly.

Not quite a family yet, I say. But now it's time for my business here, so I must raise my voice. Volunteer Kelly, we executed the wrong people for spying. I am now ordering you to rectify our company's mistake, and to execute the person who not only spied on us but who was responsible for the deaths of innocent people. Give her the same chance Bobby and Tommy got.

Her face shows no reaction: as if she's unaware of the situation, or that what I speak of has got nothing at all to do with her. When I take out the revolver, there's a movement of chairs on the floor. Martin's wife goes under the table.

Take this weapon and execute the person formerly known as Hannah Jordan. Do it at once.

There's still little or no reaction on her old face.

Kelly stands up and grabs the gun from my

hand, but instead of pointing it at his wife he turns and points it at my forehead.

Get out of here before I shoot you! His hand shakes to match the quiver in his voice — or in keeping with the rattle of crockery I'd heard earlier.

One or two other voices cry: Stop! Calm down! Don't do it!

But myself and Rutch Kelly face each other like buck cats, tails twitching, ready to lunge. It unnerves him further when I flash a smile of defiance and push my forehead against the barrel of the gun. A woman's whimpering grows louder. Kelly slides his chair with him as he steps back and moves the gun from my temple.

Do it, you cowardly bastard, I roar.

I will, I will, if you don't leave here.

As I move towards him again, he pulls the trigger. The bang is followed by a gasping sound from the others, as if a chorus is being conducted. It's hard to say whether Kelly is shocked or relieved to see me still standing before him. Shocked, he must be, because he fires again to no avail.

Before he can realize he's been conned with blanks in the gun's chambers, I swing out with my fist to catch him on the button and send him backwards. Chairs and tables crash, bodies scramble out of the way and he falls over his chair and onto the floor like he did on a cold January night long ago. I wish Mylie Byrne were here to see this.

The next minute, I'm on the floor alongside Rutch Kelly. That other son of his stands over me, and snarls. But not for long, because Martin comes up and floors him. At least the last man standing is a Rowe.

Sarah rises from the table and, ignoring the mêlée, addresses her young man. Come along, Richard, we'll leave these fiendish brutes here where they belong: for ever stuck in the middle of the Troubles; they'll never stop making a show of themselves. It's time we were gone from such a world.

The woman leads her man out the door, and we listen as their young footsteps fall hard and quickly down the flight of stairs till we can no longer hear them.

To this roomful of unease, their going at once adds an unexpected dead-quiet, the twinge of an emigrants' departure or that of a wake. In the middle of our loss, it becomes clear that without their presence all notion of fighting for whatever it is we fight, or fought, over is pointless. It feels as if the Troubles themselves were never worth it in the first place. For what good is a scrap if it doesn't clear the air and beget a future, or make no odds in the wide-earthly-world to our offspring? So myself and Rutch Kelly pull ourselves off the floor and watch each other for signs. I don't think there'll be any more bother.

For the first time, Hannah Jordan glances my way, her look one of aged contempt from over a light-blue handbag clasped under her chin, as much as to say: Now see what you've done. If only looks could talk.

I stare back at her with all the scorn I can muster: No, you see what *you've* done. You treacherous old hag, you were never worth the lead of a bullet, I tell her.

I'll let it be at that.

⋆ ⋆ ⋆

It's time to go. I must brace the beams, plumb the uprights and square my shoulders. Veering ninety degrees outside the Corner House Hotel, I'll walk in the rain, up the street and out of town. There's nothing to beat a full shower of late-September rain to green the Black Country again before winter — heaven-sent water to old roots — and it's good to see spiders mount their gauzy sails high along the ditches in wait for the next breeze to carry them off — at least they know when it's time to move on.

Ah, there you are, Lucy Brien, with your

coal-dark hair like a young one's, standing by a stile waiting for a fellow. You catch my arm there — that's it, my girl — and we'll talk about the good times. We'll relish our walk across the Bloody Bridge, through the Milehouse and up Monart hill, and bear no more grudges against spies or yeomen. Let's listen outside Robert's Forge for the old clink-clink clank, then stop at the Cutting Road and look across at what's left of Killoughrim Wood. We'll stand a while in the hallowed place, to revere instinctively the things that need revering. And may not as much as one shadow ever fall on our dreams, or, between the least expectation and how we experience it as we walk on home.